I couldn't decide whether to wait to read it, to slowly savor it, or gobble it down like a kid who hasn't had sweets in a year. Aaaaand, spoiler alert, option number 3 won out and I have no regrets. I totally binged it. It was a thrilling ride and I wish it didn't have to end! I love the Easter eggs from past Warren books and series.

MICHAELA, GOODREADS

A thrilling conclusion to a great series! Crispin's story is packed with heart pounding danger, suspense, and romance keeping you gripped to the story. Jade was the perfect match for this surprising hero with her own story and fierceness. I found this book difficult to put down yet wanting to savor every word. This series is a must read!!

MISTY, GOODREADS

Of course Susan May Warren delivers an excellent conclusion to the Chasing Fire: Montana series! Fans expect nothing less than overlapping, intense and high-stakes action, sprinkled with faith and redemption.

KIM, GOODREADS

FIREPROOF

CHASING FIRE MONTANA | BOOK 6

A SERIES CREATED BY SUSAN MAY WARREN AND LISA PHILLIPS

SUSAN MAY WARREN

sunrise
PUBLISHING

Fireproof
Chasing Fire: Montana, Book 6
Copyright © 2024 Sunrise Media Group LLC
Paperback ISBN: 978-1-963372-29-8
EBOOK: 978-1-963372-28-1

This book is a work of fiction. Names, characters, places, and
incidents are either products of the author's imagination or used
fictitiously. Any similarity to actual people, organizations, and/or
events is purely coincidental.

All Scripture quotations, unless otherwise indicated, are taken from
the King James Version.

For more information about Susan May Warren please access the
author's website at susanmawarren.com

Published in the United States of America.
Cover Design: Lynnette Bonner

Soli Deo Gloria

And Lord, haste the day when the faith shall
     be sight,
The clouds be rolled back as a scroll;
The trump shall resound, and the Lord shall
     descend,
A song in the night, oh my soul!

ONE

Frankly, Crispin was just tired of being dead.

Dead, and in his pajamas.

Wow, he needed pants, because the flimsy hospital gown was getting a little breezy.

"Thanks, Kelly," he said to the night nurse as she brought in his dinner. The ever-so-delicious red Jell-O and chicken broth. Sheesh, he still had teeth, thank you, even if his insides had been a little ground up over the past week.

That's what being kidnapped and tortured did to a guy—reduced him to slurping his food.

"Eat up. I'll be back to get your blood pressure," said Kelly. Mid-thirties, no nonsense, and in a different time, different place, he'd listen to her.

But, well, he had things to do.

He pulled the tray to himself, the IV line tugging a little on the top of his hand where it connected. "Hey. Is that cop still sitting outside my door?"

"Duane? I think he went to the cafeteria for coffee. Why? You need me to call him?" She'd stopped, her hand on the door. "Do you feel unsafe? They said he was here for your protection."

Always, but, "No. I just wanted to check on the fire and the search for my attacker."

She was pretty enough. Dark hair pulled back into a low bun, wearing teal pants and a patterned shirt, the look of a mother in her expression. She wore a ring, so probably. Now she gave him a look of pity. "No. I'm sorry. Do you want me to call the sheriff and see if he's heard anything?"

"No. That's okay." He picked up his spoon. "Thanks."

He pushed away his food, leaned his head back. Closed his eyes. So close. He'd been so, so painfully, pitifully close to wrapping up this eternal, never-ending, doggone mission.

And then a biker-gangbanger slash paid assassin named Tank had to get the drop on him and rearrange his insides, looking for answers to the question Crispin still hadn't answered — *where was the nuke?*

Good question, and really, get in line, pal. Because Crispin hadn't a clue if Two-fisted Tank was an independent world-ending terrorist or if he worked with The Brothers, a.k.a. a semiorganized Russian wannabe-terrorist group conveniently working inside the American borders — also hunting for the nuke. At this point, it was a free-for-all race to find said stolen nuclear missile, and who knew how many rogue groups might be hunting down the thief, Henry Snow?

Ex-CIA agent Henry Snow, who had rescued the nuke from the grip of a rogue CIA faction and hidden it like an easter egg in the woods of Montana. The same Henry Snow who'd reached out to Crispin three-plus months ago telling him to come to Ember, Montana.

And then promptly ghosted him.

The stupid watery broth actually smelled good. Crispin reached out to pull the tray close. Heat sheered through him up his side, where at least one rib had folded under Tank's close and personal attention.

Crispin's head still hammered too, a throb that might be more like a pellet gun against his brain thanks to the go-round he'd had with kidnapper number *dos*. This time, he'd been snatched right out of the hospital, dragged to a cabin in the woods and, from his sketchy memory, might have turned to toast in a house fire if former CIA agent, and his once-upon-a-time partner, Booth Wilder hadn't rescued him.

He remembered his floppy-meat self being dragged out of danger by Booth.

But sadly, not much more until he'd woken two days ago bandaged, IVs in one arm, on oxygen, and his entire body needing a mainline of ibuprofen.

And wearing pajamas.

Agenda item numero uno: find pants.

Then he'd have to sneak past Duane and out the door of the hospital.

Lift some wheels.

Maybe connect with Booth.

And then, finally, find Henry Snow.

Not even a clue how he'd do that.

He tasted the soup. Not terrible. He finished it, slowly, letting the heat find his bruised bones. Maybe he'd live, but he'd stopped thinking past the next five minutes.

Kelly came back in. "Oh, good. I was hoping

you'd eaten." She looked like she might hold up her hand for a fist bump.

He pushed the empty bowl and tray away but palmed the spoon and tucked it beside him. "Maybe next time add some real chicken?"

"Sorry. Not until the doc okays it. You had some pretty significant internal bleeding." As if to emphasize her words, she pulled down his blanket—

"Hey!" He put his hands on his flimsy gown. "I'm not sure what happened to my clothes, but—"

"Calm down, Mr. Lamb. I've seen it before. Besides, I'm just checking on your bruising."

Mr. Lamb. So, Booth had given the sheriff his sister's alias name. Felt right. He hadn't had a real name for years. Even Crispin was a nickname his sister had given him once upon a time.

He let Nurse Kelly check out his torso and caught a glimpse himself. Mostly black and purple, some green bruising. "That doesn't look too bad," he said.

She gaped at him. "You look like you've been hit by a buffalo, then trampled by the herd."

"Maybe just a couple of the calves—"

"And let's not forget you've been shot." She lifted the bandage that covered his shoulder. "Stitches are healing. Good thing it was a through and through."

Right. Good thing. He would have preferred *not* getting shot.

She examined his face. "At least your eye is open now. Better than when you came in three days ago. You're a fast healer."

Not fast enough. If he hadn't ached so much, he'd have sneaked out on day one.

"You know where my pants went?"

She reached for the blood pressure cuff. "Your clothes were handed over to the police for evidence."

Aw.

She finished, then took his pulse. "You're definitely on the mend. Although, you haven't had any visitors."

Yes, he had—a.k.a. his buddy Booth, who'd slipped in after visiting hours and given him the lowdown on Henry.

"Okay, so Floyd is still on the run. Still hunting Henry," Booth had said, his face illuminated by the moonlight cutting through the window. "And the nuke is still missing."

Crispin had been in too much pain to do anything but groan.

"But I think I have a lead on Henry. My uh...our team leader got tangled in a chute accident and went down in a cave. She said that Henry Snow rescued her."

That lit a fire inside him. "Where?"

"I have a rough map." Booth slipped a burner phone into his hand. "I'd given this to the sheriff, but after he told me today that Floyd was still out there..."

"I get it," Crispin said.

"I put the coordinates of where Nova met Henry in the phone. It's a cave north of here, in the Kootenai forest. The fire is still burning, though, so I need to go back out with the team."

"I got this," Crispin said. His voice sounded like he'd gargled with cement.

Booth raised an eyebrow. "We need help—"

"The minute we call anyone in is the minute the entire gang arrives, and suddenly we have the Lincoln

5

County war in Ember, Montana." He shifted and buried a groan. "I'll get out of here ASAP and find him."

Booth sighed. "You track down Henry. Then call me. Don't do this alone. I don't want to have to start a fire to save your sorry backside again." But he'd smiled. "Good to have you back, Crisp." He'd lifted a fist.

Crispin had met it. "Thanks for saving my hide."

"Twice," Booth had said. "Don't be a hero."

Right. He'd left hero behind long ago, frankly.

Now, Kelly pressed the cold face of the stethoscope to his chest. "Good news, you still have a heartbeat."

He smiled. She winked and put the scope around her neck. "Maybe another few days, and the doc will discharge you." She'd pulled out a tablet from her massive hip pocket. "I don't think the doc will let you leave without having a place to go, however."

"I have a place to go." Although, probably she meant a home, with family, so nope. Yes, his sister lived here, but he wasn't letting Tank or anyone else show up on her doorstep again, so...

"Really?" Kelly looked up from taking notes on her tablet.

"Yep. Friends in town"—sort of—"and family"—again, nope—"and I have a place north of town, well stocked." Truth. With ammo and survival supplies and everything he needed for a standoff, should the Brotherhood find him.

Again.

"My shift changes in twenty minutes, so I'll hand you off. Duane is back, but his shift is changing too." She patted Crispin's shoulder as she slipped the tablet back into her pocket. "Good thing the fire has died down in the mountains, or our bench would be leaner. Some of our nurses serve as emergency personnel on the fire line. And we're hoping for rain at the end of the week. Put an end to all this tragedy."

He nodded. "Thanks, Kelly."

She gave him a smile and picked up his tray. "See you tomorrow."

Yeah, not so much. The door closed softly behind her, and he sat up, reached for a cotton ball, and slowly pulled out his IV.

Pressed the cotton ball over the wound.

So, first thing—pants. He slipped out of bed. Then he grabbed his spoon.

Three days. Three days Floyd and his ilk had been free to hunt down Henry.

Three days. Maybe The Brothers already had the nuke.

Three days. Long enough for the Russian Bratva to set up a meet, exchange rubles for a weapon of mass destruction, and then—then it would all go down. World War Three, or at least a catastrophic terror event inside the borders of the US.

He blamed his years in the CIA for the doomsday attitude, but frankly, wasn't that what his team had given their lives to prevent? What he'd sacrificed three years of his life for?

Pants.

He poked his head out the door. Duane—big guy, clearly a Montanan with his grizzly bear girth—stood at the nurses' desk, drinking a cup of joe, chatting up the nurses: two women and a guy. Crispin remembered him—about his size, a nice guy named Nick.

7

Nick with pants that might fit him, stashed in the locker room down the hall.

Crispin waited until the nurses had all turned away, Duane's back still to him, and he slipped out the door, hugged the opposite wall, and stole down the hallway to the locker room door.

He'd spotted it earlier, during the obligatory get-out-of-bed-and-stroll portion of his recovery.

Now, he slipped inside. A clean room with a carpeted floor, showers, and wide lockers all with doors. *Locked* doors.

Aw.

But hanging on a hook on the wall was a pair of overalls, maybe from the maintenance crew. Bingo. He pulled them on, found a baseball hat in a cubby by the door, and added that over his bed-head hair.

No shoes, but he didn't have time to search.

He stuck his head back out into the hallway. No sign of Duane, so he just strolled out and headed toward the stairs. He took the steps down two flights to the emergency room.

Then he walked past a kid with a bloody nose, his arm pressed to his body, a woman holding a sleeping toddler, and right out under the canopy to the parking lot.

Darkness pressed against the arch of night, the last of the sunlight rimming the mountains to the north. Deep shadows draped the parking lot.

One unlocked car. He just needed one.

He walked around the lot, trying doors, ducking between cars, and—*jackpot*. Found a dinged-up orange Kia Rio and slid into the driver's seat.

Clearly the driver loved McDonald's. The car

reeked of French fries and the odor of sour milkshakes.

But Kias could be hotwired, and in moments, he'd used the spoon to take off the steering column. Then he found the ignition cylinder and shoved the end of the spoon in.

The car fired up.

Never mind that his bare foot stuck to the floor, something sticky on the gas pedal. He pulled out and headed into the night.

The firestorm was going to kill them all.

Jade stared out the open door of the Twin Otter at the fire that tipped the trees and chewed through the Kootenai forest below. Smoke billowed up, blackened and lethal, but Aria, the pilot, cleared a wide path around it just to give Jade and their spotter, a man named Duncan, a chance to test the wind, figure out how to deploy from the plane safely.

With the winds gusting in the thirty-mile-an-hour range, just getting her seven-person team—they were one firefighter short with Nova and another jumper named Rico out injured—out the door and onto the ground might be tricky.

But it didn't have to be pretty. Just safe.

Duncan sent out another check ribbon, and she watched it flutter out, then fall, then spiral, the storm of the fire grabbing it and turning it into a knot as it whisked it away.

It fell into the distant flames and vanished.

So, that didn't bode well.

"Take us higher, Aria," Duncan said and leaned away from the open door, holding on to his safety line.

Aria ascended, and Duncan closed the door. He spoke into his mic, and she heard it through her headphones. "Maybe we try to get west of it?"

It being the fire wall, headed south, toward civilization, chewing up downed lodgepole pine and the thick, dry loam of the tinder-dry forest. According to emergency response leader Miles Dafoe, the Jude County firefighters had waged war with the fire all summer since an explosion in the woods had first set off the blaze.

She'd read the fire reports on her tablet during her flight from Anchorage last night. Which meant she'd nabbed little sleep, although frankly, she'd learned to nap like a combat soldier after so many years fighting fires.

Her first real look at the blaze had come this morning as she'd walked into the makeshift Jude County fire center, located in a Quonset hut just off the runway.

Of course, she probably had "overachiever" stamped on her forehead. Or at least on the breast pocket of her jumpsuit. That's what happened when you dragged legacy everywhere you went.

But it didn't matter. They'd asked her to fill in as crew boss, and yeah, she planned to bring the house down. Keep the family name intact.

Make her big brother, Jed, proud. Maybe.

Of course, the heads of the top brass rose, and two of the three people smiled, something of warmth in their eyes.

"Jade." Conner Young, their supervisor, came over and held out his hand. "When did you get in?"

"Last night."

"Now I know we're in safe hands," Nova Burns, another legacy said. She grabbed Jade up in a hug.

"Conner said you needed a team lead after yours was hurt?" She stepped away. "How bad is it?"

"Hairline crack, really. I'll be fine. But it's a big fire—we need all the help we can get."

She looked over at the third man, tall, with dark hair, salty at the sides, wearing a green forest-service jumpsuit, his sleeves rolled up past his elbows. "This is our incident commander, Miles Dafoe."

He shook Jade's hand. "I know your brother only by reputation."

"That's enough of a threat," she said, and Miles smiled.

But she wasn't exactly kidding, was she?

Miles then pointed to a screen where a drone flew over the acres and acres of burning forest. A man who seemed in his late twenties worked the controls like he might be in a video game.

"The fire started last night—one of our pilots called it in this morning," Miles said. "We're currently fighting a blaze that's burned nearly all of central Kootenai, all the way over to County Road 518. It took out the campground and Wildlands Academy fire camp, and it even came close to a couple ranches, although we were able to save them."

He ran his hand over a map of the massive Kootenai mountain area, spread out on a wall. Tiny yellow pushpins indicated firefighters still out in the field.

"We have the fire corralled, but it's not over. And now, with this new fire pushing in from the east"—he ran a finger up South Fork Road—"if these two

11

combine, we'll have a conflagration we won't be able to put down. It could reach Snowhaven." He ran his hand down to a red pushpin about ten miles north of Ember.

"I've been there a few times," Jade said. "Tourist town. Real population less than a thousand."

"Yes. And if the blaze gets past Snowhaven, it heads right to Ember."

"Looks like HQ already had a fire." She glanced over at the half-burnt HQ building, the front section demolished, the back draped with tarps and temporary shelter.

"Arsonist. Long story," said Conner. "But right now our focus is knocking down this fire before it joins forces with the main blaze."

"My, or rather, *your* team is ready to go," Nova said. She leaned a little on a crutch, her ankle wrapped. "They've been in for forty-eight hours—the hotshots are out with the blaze. But that area is inaccessible except by plane so—"

"Yep," Jade said. "So, we have Flattail Creek to the west, and generally, we just need to cut the fire off to the south."

"Yes. There's a small lake here—Rainbow Lake. And a creek that runs east-west. Get in, fortify a line along the creek, and use it to help slow down the blaze. We'll attack the head, too, with slurry and water from the lake, and if we can knock it down, then it's one less thing to worry about."

"What's the wind like?" Her gut tightened on the answer.

"Northwest."

Right. "I'll meet the team on the tarmac."

Nova left, and Jade loaded up her jump pockets

with a couple maps, a walkie, extra batteries, and then headed to the locker room to grab a gear bag—water, gloves, a fire shelter, space blanket, two days of MREs, a flare, and a knife. She'd already grabbed a helmet and a Pulaski and now climbed into her jumpsuit, a heavy canvas outer layer that would protect her from the heat and flames.

Should she land in the fire.

She blew out a breath. She hadn't done that since…well, since she'd been a *rookie*.

The team waited for her at the plane, doing buddy checks on their equipment. She met the pilot—Aria, dark hair, no-nonsense—and the rest of the team. Orion and Vince, a couple sawyers, and Logan, her team lead, and JoJo, a woman who also had a bit of legacy on her tail.

They got in, and Nova stood on the tarmac and waved, her face a little twisted. Yeah, Jade got that. Her worst nightmare might be sending her team out without her.

And that sounded arrogant, but they were her responsibility. And a Ransom didn't let their team down.

Thank you, big bro, for that rep.

But Jade was all in, even now, an hour later, as she stared out at the fire consuming Flatiron Mountain. It had burned around the base, approximately three miles from Rainbow Lake, and was heading southwest fast.

"Okay," she said to Duncan. "We're going to drop closer to the lake and set up along the creek. I know it's a farther hike, but there's a nice bald spot just north, and it's away from the fire." She looked at her crew, kitted up, strapped into their safety lines. "Nobody dies today."

Logan, her second-in-command, gave her a thumbs-up.

The plane banked, and Aria brought them around. Logan scooted up to Jade. "I can be first stick out with JoJo."

Not a bad idea, given the wind. If someone got blown off course, she could track them. Although, rules were, at least on her team in Alaska, crew chief went out the door first.

And she hated breaking the rules.

Still, safety first. She nodded, and as Aria descended and Duncan opened the door, Logan and JoJo lined up, first stick.

Duncan sent out a ribbon, and she watched it, her jaw tight as it fell. He looked at her and shot her a thumbs-up.

She nodded, and Logan and JoJo went out the door as she leaned over, a gloved hand on her safety line, watching.

Two chutes, deployed.

Orion and Vince jumped next. Two more chutes.

She stepped up to the door, watching.

The wind grabbed at them, but both Orion and Vince maneuvered with their toggles.

Duncan unhooked her safety line. "Be safe!"

She nodded—and jumped.

Air, brisk and full, and this—*this* was the moment that caught her up every time. The freedom, the expanse of the moment swept through her, stole her breath, told her that she might be invincible, and right now, she believed it.

Jump thousand.

Below, the flames reached for her, snapping, the wind kicking up. Logan and JoJo had already landed, a nice touchdown maybe a half mile from the blaze.

Look thousand.

She got the lay of the land—the mountain to the north, rising tall and bald, although it had nothing on the jagged beauty of the Alaska Range. A service road to the east, running northwest, cutting through the forest, a brown ribbon.

Reach thousand.

To the west, the glistening blue of the Flattail River, some twenty feet wide in areas, narrower in others. Enough, maybe, to stop the blaze.

As she drifted down, she made out a few landmarks. Wildlands Academy to the west, burnt. There went a summer full of memories.

Wait thousand.

Smoke hurtled up toward her—she'd drifted a little over the fire, the furnace tugging at her. Vince and Orion had touched earth, also in the bald spot. She glanced at the fire and pulled her rip cord.

Pull thousand.

Maybe a little soon, but the chute billowed out and caught with a jerk and a shot of pain she'd come to expect.

Then she settled into her harness and reached for the toggles.

Nothing.

She looked up. The toggles had wrapped around the risers, caught on the links. Reaching up, she caught one, tried to untangle it.

Focus. Breathe.

But the storm grabbed her, tossed her away from her trajectory.

Don't look down.

Nope. Not a chance. Below her, the fire snapped, roared, still some thousand feet below, but—

She got the toggle free. Looped it through her arm and reached for the other. No good—it was knotted around the link, not a hope of release.

The fire below her roared.

She reefed down hard on her right toggle, and the chute arched to the right, over the fire. *C'mon, c'mon.* She kept reefing, and the rig kept turning, heading east now.

She let off on the reef, and the chute straightened out, flying away from the bald spot, falling, the fire beneath her.

Still hungry.

But wind—maybe the breath of God—caught her, and she sailed over the exploding treetops, the smoke coughing up around her. Her eyes burned, but she spotted the road—

Wait. As she crossed over it, headed for the trees, she made out a car—an orange car in the ditch, the front end crushed against an electrical pole. Broken at the impact, the pole had flattened the top of the little car and fallen into the forest on the opposite side, the forest burnt and crispy.

Source of fire solved.

And then—trees. She braced herself and curled her legs up to protect them as she fell into the tangle of trees, hitting branches and crashing through leaves until she jerked, hard. Her breath shook out, her harness burned against her thighs.

She hung, swinging in the tree, some thirty feet from the forest floor.

So much for a glorious, epic first day on the job.

TWO

So much for his brilliant escape from the hospital. At this rate, he'd perish, alone and trapped in a car, and they'd find his emaciated, decaying body...well, maybe never, given the remoteness of his location.

Maybe Crispin wouldn't starve to death. He'd die from exposure, or even blood loss—his shoulder wound having ripped open—one drip at a time as he struggled to free himself from his prison.

From what he could make out, the tree he'd crashed into had flattened the tiny Kia.

If he could just reach the stupid burner phone, which had flown off his seat into the depths of the vehicle...

For the fiftieth time, as if the phone fairies might have decided to move the phone into his reach, he stretched out his free hand and felt around the debris-ridden floor of the car. Cups, wrappers, and who knew what sort of grossness lay in the litter.

Empty.

He laid his head back down on the seat, trying to unravel the crash. Most of it came up blank, but he did remember seeing a deer in his headlights. Remembered hitting the brakes.

He'd woken up, smashed against the passenger seat on his side, his legs tangled in the steering wheel, his body curled under the passenger dashboard, the roof pressing against his shoulder and legs.

He ached, but nothing felt broken. He'd managed to squeeze himself up to the passenger seat. Tried the door. Of course, stuck.

And then the acrid odor of smoke filled the cab, along with a tiny glow of red light against the spidery glass of the crushed windshield. He'd waited most of the night for the fire to consume him, to light the haze of gasoline that filled the car.

Now, as the morning misted into the car, a chill ran through his body. He had worked one leg free of the crushed driver's side, but he hadn't a hope of getting that door open.

Sorry, Booth. And Sophie, who had never really gotten a chance to get to know him again after his three-year stint of playing dead. She'd deserved more than his quick *Hello! I'm alive!* and a hug before he was back on the trail of The Brothers and the missing nuke.

Although, in truth, she'd known he wasn't dead. He'd sent her postcards for years, secret hints as to his non-demise, so he wasn't a complete jerk. Mostly.

This stupid job had cost him more than he'd ever expected. Including, apparently, a hero's death. No, he'd go down as the guy taken out by Bambi.

He didn't *think* he'd hit the deer, but that sounded about right—people and things that came into his headlights often ended up dead.

"Hello!"

He jerked, looked up toward the sliver of glass that remained of the passenger window.

"Anyone in there—"

"Yes!" He jerked, and of course banged his head on the ceiling of the crushed roof, adding sparks to his already pounding head. "I'm here!"

"Oh my gosh—okay, listen, I'm going to try and get your door open."

He loved that idea. Except—"With what, the handy jaws of life in your glove box?" Because he hadn't heard a siren. He could only guess she might be a passerby, had glimpsed the crumpled orange Kia in the ditch.

Or maybe an angel, sent by God, showing up to save him, just like his mother always said. *A very present help in times of trouble*, although that hadn't exactly worked out for her, had it?

"Shield your eyes. I'm not sure how this glass will break."

He buried his face in the crook of his arm as the door creaked, fighting whatever wedge she'd put into the space. Putting his hand on the door, he tried to help, to unlatch it, to push with her force.

The door wrenched open with a shriek. Fresh air poured in, and a woman crouched at the opening. She wore a helmet, a yellow Nomex jacket, and held a Pulaski.

A firefighter. Sounded right, given the wildland fire that burned around them.

"You're bleeding." Her sunglasses hid her eyes, and she looked like a bandit with her handkerchief around her neck. Her dark-blonde hair hung in a single utilitarian braid. She put down the axe. "I have a first aid kit—"

"Get me out of here first. Don't worry about the blood—that's an old wound."

"Huh," she said, but grabbed his upper arms with her gloved hands. He was already working himself free, gritting his teeth against the burn in his leg. So maybe he'd only been numb to whatever broken bones—

Nope. Not broken, just stuck, and as he wrenched himself free, he ripped his pants and maybe sliced open some skin but managed to tumble out onto the soft, loamy earth. Gasoline from his destroyed tank soaked the ground, and he dragged himself away, with the woman's help.

Which he shook free of as soon as he found his legs.

He stood up, and—oops, head rush—braced himself on a nearby tree.

"You should sit down," she said.

His knees were already obeying.

She uncapped a canteen and handed it over. He took it, drinking too greedily—because maybe she needed it, but his entire body suddenly craved water.

"That's a pretty nasty scrape there," said the woman, who had taken the liberty of examining his leg. "And let me get a look at that shoulder wound."

"I'm fine," Crispin said, wiping his arm across his mouth.

She leaned back. "Clearly not. You have a head wound, and your face is pretty beat up, and you're bleeding and—"

"Thanks for the rescue." Only then did he see that the fire burned on the opposite side of the dirt road, the "tree" an electrical pole. Awesome. He'd lit an entire forest on fire.

More collateral damage. He was attaining epic status.

He pushed himself up. Oops, no go. His head spun, and again he grabbed a tree limb. She stood up and steadied him, her hand on his arm. "Let me radio in for help. See if we can get a chopper out here."

He shook his head. "I'm good. My place is just up the road. I just need—" He'd taken a step and clenched his jaw against a groan.

"What you need is medical attention."

He turned to her and got a good look at her. Blood scraped her jawline, and she leaned a little on her Pulaski. "So do you."

"I'm fine." Clearly she had a case of the Crispins.

He gave a laugh that had nothing to do with humor. "Right. What happened? You get hit by a tree spur?" It happened—the snags from burnt trees came down on firefighters working the line.

"My chute got caught in the trees. I had to lower myself down. Not enough rope."

Which meant she'd had to jump the last bit to the bottom, probably, hence the tender ankle? "What's your name?"

"Jade. Yours?"

He sighed. Why not? "Crispin. Where's the rest of your team?" He took another swig of water, then handed her back the canteen.

"Other side of Flatiron Mountain. West of the fire. My chute malfunctioned."

She said it like it might just be another Tuesday, no hint of panic in her voice. Interesting. She lifted her glasses away and tucked them in the brim of her yellow helmet. Pretty eyes—brown, with hints of gold.

"It'll take a bit for me to get picked up—too much attention on knocking down the fire. Which you started, I think." She raised a brow.

He didn't know why that irked him. "Yeah, I did that on purpose. Because there hasn't been enough fire around here."

"I was just stating a fact."

"Here's another fact. There was a deer. I swerved. The electrical pole got in my way. Thanks for the save." He took a step. Fire burned up his leg, but it didn't give out. And he didn't wobble.

"How far is your place?" She followed him, as if to catch him.

"Could be a mile, up the road and to the east."

"Perfect. Let's go."

He stilled. "I can make it."

"Listen, I have to call in for a ride anyway. I usually carry a tracker, but...anyway, I can't seem to get radio reception, so I'm on the hunt for cell service. I can't in good conscience let a clearly injured man limp off into the woods alone, so—"

"I'm not limping."

"You're practically staggering."

He opened his mouth. Closed it. "Yeah, well, you're not running any marathons." He indicated her near-limp as she took a step toward him.

"Bet I could outrun you."

His eyebrow rose. Shoot, now he sort of liked her.

"Okay, hotshot, try and keep up. You can call in a ride with my sat phone."

Phone.

He headed back to the car. Yes, staggering a little. Perfect.

Kneeling, he reached around the twisted carcass

of the seat. There. Hopefully it wasn't a dried-up hamburger bun.

Nope. He pulled out his burner phone. But his swiped overalls didn't contain a pocket.

"Give it to me," said Jade.

He handed it over, and she put it in her leg pouch.

"And I'm a smokejumper, not a hotshot." Then she stepped right up to him and put her hand around his waist. "Put a sock in it, Crispy. You need help."

Crispy?

He didn't push her away, however, because she just might be right. For now, as they picked their way to the road and as she used her Pulaski to balance them, he'd hold on.

They were a pair, hobbling up the dirt road together, bloodied, the forest blackened on one side, the haze of smoke in the air.

All he could think was...this was a bad, very bad idea. Because who knew if The Brothers had found his house? Already gotten into his weapons cache. Maybe set up a perimeter, watching the screens in his office or even from inside his garage-bunker, ready to pick him and his come-along off as they stumbled into his compound.

Or worse, waiting to capture him again—no, capture *them*—and then he'd get to watch as another in-his-periphery victim got tortured and murdered.

He should probably ditch this woman before being in his airspace got her killed. But she had a pretty good grip on him, and frankly, everything hurt, so...

So he just prayed—yes, *prayed*, because he'd never fully jettisoned the hope his mother was right. That indeed, God hadn't abandoned him, despite evidence to the contrary.

And that this time, *please*, he wasn't walking into an ambush, taking pretty Jade the Smokejumper with him.

Jade had lied.

That fact only worsened with every step. Because Jade had landed hard—too hard—on her ankle coming out of that tree, and every step made her want to yelp, but…

But Crispin—she still couldn't believe she'd called him Crispy—had gotten under her skin a little with his I-don't-need-help-even-though-I'm-bleeding-and-can-barely-walk attitude. How she hated tough guys. So he needed her, and if he thought she might be hurt, he'd be the one insisting on carrying her.

She'd met too many tough guys—ahem, her brother Jed, and maybe her entire Midnight Sun firefighting crew, along with various SAR types that seemed to congregate in the last frontier state—so she knew how they operated.

Always had to be the hero.

This hero happened to be walking in bare feet too. She'd noticed as soon as she'd pulled him from the crumpled car, but he'd said nothing, so she hadn't either.

But, weird.

"How much farther?" she said, keeping the pain out of her voice. Because she could do hero too if she had to.

"There's a drive just up ahead, and the cabin is

about five hundred yards in." His voice emerged a little tight, so she guessed he might still be in more pain than her. Probably, he could be suffering from exposure, too, the temps last night having dropped despite the summer air. Given the state of his face, he'd hit the dash pretty hard, although some of the bruising looked faded—

Old wound, he'd said. Bar fight? But she didn't smell alcohol on him. He was wearing overalls, so a working man—maybe a plumber. One who'd lost his shoes? He wore a scruff of a dark-brown beard, and his body, despite the weakness, seemed lean and strong. His arm was draped over her shoulder, and he stood maybe eight inches taller than her, so she guessed around six three. He did have interesting eyes—hazel-green with flecks of gold, and a look in them that suggested pain along with a hint of anger. Clearly hiding something.

Maybe that story about the deer running him off the road. Except, again, no liquor smell. It didn't matter. He needed help, and she needed a phone. Or a signal.

Mostly, she needed to get back to her team.

As if reading her mind, he said, "So, you're with the Jude County smokejumpers?"

Interesting. But probably, with the summer of fire, everyone knew the JC fire team. "I'm just here to fill in as crew chief while the other one is on the mend. Came down from my team in Alaska. Although, I'm familiar with Ember. My brother, Jed, was the crew chief for a hotshot crew for years here. He's down in Missoula for the summer with my sister-in-law, Kate, who was another Ember legacy firefighter. I'm bunking at his place while I'm here."

They turned down the dirt road, the grass high between the tire trails. "How long have you lived here?"

"Not long. It's just up ahead." He'd slowed, however, seemed to be scanning the area as if— "Actually, how about if you hang back for a second—"

"What, you have an ornery hound dog that's going to bite me?"

"Something like that." He lifted his arm from her shoulder. Scanned the area. Between the trees sat a small cabin with a front porch, surrounded by towering Douglas firs, set in the middle of a cleared-out swath of land. A small outbuilding that looked like a garage. A woodbin and a grill sat on the porch, along with one Adirondack chair.

So, the guy lived alone.

He took a step, grunted, and that was just *enough*.

"Oh, for Pete's sake. I can handle a dog." She put her arm back around his waist. "C'mon." She practically dragged him into his yard, his arm tighter around her.

He picked up his pace then and hustled her to the front door. Despite the rustic exterior, it held a keypad, and he keyed in a code.

The door unlocked, and he practically shoved her inside.

Pulled the door shut behind him and locked it.

"You're not a serial killer, are you? Because I do know how to use this." She held up her axe.

"Just stay away from the windows."

Huh?

Small but clean. A big room with a wooden planked floor covered in a braided wool rug, a worn

27

but comfy-looking leather sofa in the middle of the room, and a potbellied stove that sat on stones in the corner. Behind that, a small kitchen held a table in the center, a pantry to one side, and a small vintage fridge and stove to the other. The sink overlooked the forested backyard.

He disappeared into one of the two rooms off the main.

She followed him in.

Stilled.

Monitors hung on the wall—six of them—and he must have tapped into some underground electrical line, because they all hummed with pictures of every angle of the yard, including the drive. Now she tightened her grip on the Pulaski. "Are you some sort of prepper?"

He had fired up his computer that sat on a simple wooden table and now studied the screens. "Something like that."

She picked up her radio, turned it on.

"Wait."

He walked over to her, and she stepped back, held up her axe.

"Wait for what? You to drug me and shove me into your basement? You're right—this was a bad idea. I'll just step outside—"

"You're not going anywhere."

And with that, the tiny hairs on the back of her neck stood on end. "I think I am, buddy—"

He held up his hands, and just like that, his expression changed. "Oh, wow. Sorry. Um...okay." He swallowed. "There are people after me, and I thought maybe they'd staked out the house. I'm not sure they haven't, but…" He let out a breath. "Let's get some ice on your ankle. I know you're limping."

He did?

She didn't move.

"I really promise that I'm not a murderer living in the woods."

"That's what a murderer in the woods would say."

He smiled at that. Shoot, he had a nice smile. A non-killer-in-the-woods smile. And when he added the smallest twinkle in his eyes, he was almost handsome. A John Krasinski action hero kind of handsome. "Yep," he said. "So I guess you'll just have to trust me."

She narrowed an eye but moved back to let him pass. He headed to the kitchen and pulled an ice pack from the inner freezer of the ancient green fridge. Handed it to her.

"You keep this at the ready?"

He lifted a shoulder.

"Because of your MMA side gig?"

He raised an eyebrow. She held up a flattened hand and waved it in a circle in front of his face. "You have a sort of Conor McGregor post-bout look about you. I have a hard time believing the steering wheel fought back."

Another twitch of his mouth. But he walked over to a small room, opened the door. Bathroom.

She sat on one of the straight-back kitchen chairs and undid her boot. This could be a bad idea, given the swelling might make it impossible to put her boot back on. But, ice. She eased it off, closing one eye.

The water ran in the next room, and after a moment, during which she put her foot up and iced her ankle, he came out, a little cleaner.

And with his shirt off.

So, not a plumber. Or maybe the fittest plumber she'd ever met, not an inch of fat on his toned, ripped torso, a smattering of black hair dusting his chest. But oh. My. The guy had certainly taken some McGregor hits, his torso blackened with old blood, green and still purple in areas. A bandage at his shoulder spotted with dried blood. She leaned back. Folded her arms. "Who are you?"

"Just a guy. Ran into trouble in town. But...I need you to take a look at my stitches." He turned and, yep, blood ran down his back. He'd taken off the bandage, revealing a small, puckered seam of skin, stitched. Blood had escaped the edges. "Are they ripped?"

He crouched, and she leaned in to examine the wound. And it hit her—"Is this a *gunshot* wound?"

"Are they ripped?"

"Yes, a couple. But the rest are intact."

"Tape it up." He held a roll of medical tape over his shoulder.

"Who are you? Jason Bourne?" She ripped the tape and then closed the open parts, pulling one edge into the next.

"Nope." He stood. Took the tape. "Just a murderer in the woods." He winked.

Aw, she didn't know what to believe.

He disappeared into the other room—probably his bedroom, because he came out with a pair of shorts and a black T-shirt. Paused. "There's a sat phone in the office. Feel free to call your team."

Right.

Then he disappeared again into the bathroom. A moment later, the shower ran.

Her ankle throbbed less, although she still gritted her teeth as she got up and headed to the office.

Conner answered her call on the first ring. "Chief Young."

"It's me, Jade—"

"Where in the Sam Hill are you? The team is losing their minds."

"I'm fine. Chute malfunction, and I got blown into the trees. No radio service, but I'm calling from a cabin. It's off South Fork Road, maybe ten miles from Ember, east of the jump site. And I repeat, I'm fine. But I found an injured motorist. We both need pickup, but it's not urgent."

The shower had turned off.

"Okay, I'll get someone to get up there and pick you up. You okay to sit tight for a bit? Could be tonight, even."

"The fire's that bad?"

"The wind stirred up the main blaze to the west, although your team is working fast. Logan's at the helm."

"Everybody okay?"

"Now they are."

Right.

"I'll be in touch." He hung up.

"Hungry?"

She turned, and Crispin slash Bourne stood at the door, the black shirt stuck to his body, his dark hair tousled with the towel he held in his hands, shorts on. He'd done a quick shave, leaving only stubble on his angular face. A line of blood trickled from his shin, the scrape a shallow line, not needing stitches. Just another rip in his fine exterior.

Frankly, she couldn't decide if he looked fierce and invincible or just barely holding himself together.

"I could eat." She got up.

"I hope you like eggs—"

A gunshot took out the glass of his front window, and just like that, Crispin took her down, his body over hers, his hands braced on either side of her.

What—

She gasped, but he moved—faster than his body seemed capable of—rolling and scrambling to his office. "Stay down!"

Another shot and absolutely, no problem, she was down, down! But she would scramble behind the sofa, thank you, because—"What is going on!"

He emerged from the office, holding—seriously? —an AR-15.

Which seemed way too appropriate for a murderer in the woods.

He hunkered down at his broken window and fired. "We're under attack."

Of course they were.

THREE

How had The Brothers found him already? He'd checked the monitors—

Aw, it didn't matter. Because trouble had a homing beacon on him, and of course they'd found him. And now Jade too.

"Get down!" he shouted again as she peeked her head over the sofa.

"I'm down, for Pete's sake. Who is shooting at us?"

He crouched in front of the window, staring out at the front line of woods. What he needed was his infrared thermal scope. But he couldn't leave the window.

"I see them!" Jade's voice came from the office. Stubborn woman!

"What are you doing? I told you to stay down!"

"There's one behind that trio of birch, one o'clock."

He scanned the forest through his viewfinder, spotted the birch trees. "Gotcha." A man dressed in fatigues, bearded, holding an AK-47, of course.

Probably supplied by their Russian cohorts. Crispin pulled the trigger.

"You got him."

He took a breath. "See anyone else?"

A beat. His neck ached with the whiplash of standing in the doorway and trying to get his brain around the sight of a pretty smokejumper sitting in his cabin, then hunkering down in a firefight, the same pretty smokejumper feeding him intel.

Who was this girl?

"Yes. Another shooter. He might be out of eyesight. He's at your nine o'clock, way over by the garage."

He shifted and then ducked as another shot brought down the rest of the glass in the window. Hey! Windows were expensive. He let out a breath, ran his sight slowly from the garage to the woods.

There. Wearing a bandanna over his mouth and nose, a grimy gimme hat, jeans, and a vest. Crispin dropped him.

Silence.

"Did I—"

"Yep," she said, her voice closer, and he looked up to see her standing at the doorway, her expression stripped. "You killed him."

He nodded, lowered the gun. A beat passed between them, and his brain ran over the hopefully tongue-in-cheek accusation from earlier—murderer in the woods.

Whoops.

"Who were those guys? And who are you? And no lying this time." She stood with her hands on her hips.

And he hadn't really realized how pretty she was,

not until this moment—with her brown eyes sparking and her blonde hair yanked from its braid, falling around her shoulders. She stood a little over a half foot shorter than him, especially without her boots on, and had curves under that forest service uniform.

A little spitfire, clearly.

He nearly smiled at the fire reference in his head.

She, however, cocked her head and raised an eyebrow.

He glanced out the window. "You're sure they're gone?"

"Not even a little, but your Batcave setup in there doesn't register any more heat sources on the screen, so spill there, Batman."

He sorta, weirdly, preferred Crispy.

And maybe he could skirt around the edges of truth. At the least, it might keep her safe to know the danger that lurked in the woods. "For the past few years, I've been hunting down a rogue militia in our country called The Brothers. They're aligned with a particularly dangerous faction of the Russian Bratva—"

"The mob?"

"Yes, although according to chatter on the dark web, they're affiliated with a Russian general who wants nothing more than to draw America into another war with Russia."

"Why?"

"Money. Power. Politics. Anyway, about four months ago, one of my old contacts reached out and told me to come to Montana. I discovered that this area is a hotbed of Brothers activity led by a guy named Floyd Blackwell. His brother, Earl, was killed earlier this summer, and since then, it's gotten personal."

She tightened her arms around her waist, and he didn't miss the glance at her Pulaski, still leaned up to the table. "Did you kill him? Earl?"

He met her eyes. "No, I did not. He died in the fire."

She swallowed, nodded.

"I'm telling the truth. Not that it matters to Floyd. He put out a hit on me and…" And oops, he'd nearly blown Booth's cover. "And then got the jump on me."

"He shot you."

"No, that was…that was a guy named Tank, but Floyd tried to finish the job."

"He did all that." She pointed to his torso. "Boot prints."

He nodded. "That was three days ago. He's been out here ever since, maybe waiting for me. I should go out in the yard and identify —"

"Have you lost your mind?" She advanced toward him. "You're not going out there!"

"Um —"

"I'm calling Conner, and I'm going to send the sheriff up here —"

"No." He stood up. "That's a bad —"

The world spun, hit him hard at an angle. He put out a hand to the wall, braced himself.

"Are you shot again?"

He winced, then braced his hand on a chair and sank into it. "Concussion. A couple days ago, but my headache won't go away." He leaned his head back, and it only made it worse.

In fact…

He pushed himself up from the chair, reached for

the sofa, and then she was there, holding on to him as he fought his way to the bathroom.

"Leave me—" he said at the door and then closed it on her before he lost it.

Aw, there went what was left of the chicken broth. Afterwards, he leaned against the cool tile wall, sweating. Shoot, clearly all this exertion had him going into shock, maybe.

"All done?" she said. "Because I'm coming in."

He tried to brace his foot to the door, but she jammed it open. Looked down at him. Shook her head. "Tough guys drive me crazy."

Huh?

She grabbed a towel, wetted it, and crouched in front of him, pressing it to his face. Her hand against his forehead followed it. "You're hot. Like you have a fever."

"I'm fine."

"You're so far from fine you can't even see it in the rearview mirror." She braced her legs on either side of his hips, then reached down and grabbed his armpits. "Up we go, big guy. Let's get you on the sofa, get your feet up. Nobody dies on my watch."

He scrabbled up and somehow managed not to rip the towel bar from the wall. But he didn't fight her as she helped him to the sofa. Crashing down onto it, he grunted, bracing himself for the heat that seemed to consume him. The cloth centered him, the coolness of it pulling fire from his brain.

Or maybe that was just her hand on his cheek.

"Don't sleep," she said.

"Mm-hmm." But his eyes closed.

"Oh, this is going to be fun." She got up and headed to the kitchen. More running water, the sound of ice dropping into a bowl, and she returned, cold, wet rag swimming in frigid water.

He groaned, something of wretched pleasure, when she wrung it out and put it on his head. Then she picked up his wrist and took his pulse.

"Well, that'll win the Kentucky Derby. You need to breathe, slow everything down."

"I don't do slow," he mumbled.

"Today you do." She moved his bare feet to the arm of the sofa, raised them. "Wanna tell me how you lost your shoes?"

Shoes? Oh, right. "I broke out of the hospital. They took my clothes. And my shoes." He opened one eye to see her shaking her head. "Listen, I'm not sure how everything got so out of hand, but I'm not...I'm not normally—"

"Such a disaster?" She pulled up a chair, took the rag, got it cold again, and returned it—thank you, sweet heaven—to his head. "I hope not. How did you live this long without me?"

She was kidding. Of course she was kidding. But right now, any answer had been stripped from his head. He made a sound—could be agreement, could be laughter, he didn't know. Definitely not argument, especially as she got up and went to the fridge again. "You have eggs."

"I like eggs," he mumbled.

"Just eggs."

"There's a ribeye in the freezer."

The door opened, closed, and something smacked the counter.

"Okay, Tough Guy. Stay alive and I'll cook for you."

"No promises," he mumbled.

"You'd better be kidding."

He said nothing, and clearly that ignited something, because she appeared over the edge of the sofa.

"I'm serious. I have a zero-casualty rate as a crew chief, and I'd like to keep it that way."

"Yes, ma'am."

She smiled. And weirdly, it seemed to reach down inside him, jump-start something dormant and even forgotten inside.

Something that might just keep him alive.

"Good. Now, tell me. Have you always been this much trouble?"

"Mm-hmm."

"I'm going to need words." She disappeared to the kitchen again.

"Always. Trouble." Probably further back than he wanted to admit.

She came back, this time with a glass of water. Sat on the sofa beside him and held up his head. "Drink."

"What is this, whiskey?"

"Do you want whiskey? I looked, but I didn't see anything."

He took a sip, then another, and leaned away before he started coughing. "I don't drink."

"Good. There's only so much trouble a girl can handle." She put his head down, back on the arm.

"So, start at the beginning, Tough Guy, and tell me how you became a DC hero."

He looked at her, sitting there beside him, a smile trying to mask the concern on her face, and the last thing he wanted was to tell her about his miserable three years of darkness, and maybe even the tragedy before that, so, "Nope."

She cocked her head.

"You should leave me. Get away from here." He looked away from her.

She sighed. "Probably. But for now, I'm in it to win it. And I don't leave a teammate behind."

"Teammate?"

"Should I say *pardner*?" She added a twang. "Besides, if there are any more gunslinging *brothers* in the woods, I think I'll sit tight."

He sighed, so deep his ribs burned. "Why are you making this so hard?"

"What? Letting you die here, alone in the woods? I don't know, maybe you're cute."

"I am not cute."

She laughed. "It *is* hard to tell under all those bruises."

"Still not an answer."

Her smile dimmed. "Because I left someone once, and I'm not doing it again."

The last—very last—thing she should do was let Crispin inside. Except, too late, because the man had this way of looking at her like she might hold his belay line, and frankly...

Frankly, she liked it.

In fact, it seemed he almost liked her.

As in, *liked* her.

Crazy. She'd simply shut down all her flirting receptors for so long she didn't know how to read a guy. Especially a guy who had been knocked upside the head one too many times. So clearly, he couldn't be trusted to be in his right mind.

Still, when he'd met her gaze, not smiling, with his not-an-answer reply, so much intensity in those hazel-green eyes…she'd found her mouth speaking, maybe her *heart* speaking, before her brain could engage.

"You did it once?" he said now, his voice soft, his eyes open. "Left someone to die?"

She drew in a breath. "Never mind. It's not—"

"Listen. You want me to stay awake? You have to do the heavy lifting, Jade the Smokejumper."

Oh. Fine. "A couple years ago, one of my teammates was hurt on a jump. He was on my stick, so I was responsible for him. He landed wrong, and I saw it. He said he was fine—even got up with his gear and followed us out to the line. But in my gut, I knew something wasn't right."

She removed his cloth, sank it into the cold water. He seemed less feverish, but it could be the residue of the cold water. He was breathing better, so maybe she'd forestalled the shock.

Still, he shouldn't sleep.

"We were working on the side of a mountain, cutting a line at the base, getting ready for an indirect attack and a backfire."

"Which is?"

"We start a fire along the line and let it burn out the area before the front wall of the main fire arrives, thus depleting the fire's fuel. We dig the line, control the smaller fire, and it kills the bigger fire." She put the cloth back on his head. Sat back.

"We were at the bottom of a hill, with a forest service road behind us. We'd spread out, digging, and then our chief called for the drip torches to start the spot fires. It was only after we'd started the fire and were ready to head to safety that I realized Griffin

41

hadn't caught up. The firestorm had caught the flames, and smoke clouded the mountain, and we couldn't see anything. I ran up the cut line and eventually spotted him. He had collapsed just outside the cut line, clearly in pain. And the fire had jumped his line. I called it in, but by then the fire had cut us off from the team, so we tried to get to the road. That's when the fire blew up."

He hadn't taken his eyes off her, and they widened now.

"We had to deploy our fire shelters. But we weren't in the clear, so we had to dig out holes—anyway, it could have been worse. Our team found us and doused the fire, but only after it had torched the ground around us."

She swallowed then, caught in the vortex of memory, the heat, and Griffin shouting in the shelter next to her.

"Griffin, because of his injury, couldn't keep his shelter down. He suffered third-degree burns on his leg."

"And you?"

"Just...minor. The fire got in around my elbows, my knees, but nothing out of the ordinary."

"Out of the—this happens a lot?"

She pointed to his face. "This happen a lot?"

He narrowed his eyes. "Ninja move there."

She lifted a shoulder. "Yes, we sometimes get burned. But if I hadn't left him on the line—when he said he was *okay* and told me to leave—then he wouldn't be walking around with scars today."

Crispin's gaze didn't leave her as she reached over for his washcloth. But his hand caught her wrist.

"You're not to blame for another person's stubbornness."

She paused, then leaned in, lowered her voice, her eyes in his. "Pride goeth before the fall."

A beat, and he let her go, then smiled. "Okay, Jade the Smokejumper, you win. Has anyone told you that you're a little bossy?"

"I'd classify it as *right*." She took away the cloth. "But most of it is just wanting to make sure that everyone makes it home. Actually, I had a friend in my dorm during undergrad who developed a tracking device you could wear on your finger. It's a ring, but it connects to GPS. You download the app on your phone. I saw her last summer in Alaska—Tae's dating a guy who's from there—and she was working on an updated prototype. Gave me one, to test it. I should have worn it today." She shook her head. "I'm working on a version for jumpers, something flexible yet easy to wear under their gloves. That way if they get separated, we can find them. There's no fire that is worth the life of a teammate."

She dipped the washcloth into the water. "And even this gang. Certainly they can't be worth all this."

He breathed in, wincing. "Some things are worth giving everything we have," he said quietly and then looked away.

She so wanted to follow that comment down the road to answers, but the set of his jaw turned her silent.

"My brother believed that," she finally said, quietly. "At least, until he and the woman he loved got caught in a fire."

He looked back at her. "That's right. You said your brother was a firefighter."

43

"Sort of a legend among the firefighting community in the Lower 48. Hence why I planted my stake in Alaska."

"That's where you live?"

"Just in the summer. In the winter, I work for the Bureau of Land Management, in their fire sciences department. I have a masters in fire science, and we're working on some virtual reality training programs to better prepare our crew chiefs."

"So, you're like the special forces of firefighting."

"Not really, but…" She lifted a shoulder. "Maybe."

"Did your brother get you into this?"

"Jed? Not even a little. He hated that I fought fires. I attended Wildlands Academy one summer— ended up with the Top Firefighter award, and he wouldn't talk to me the entire drive home. I think he's still mad at me."

Crispin frowned. "Why?"

And nope, she wasn't going there. Because she couldn't bear for him to look at her as damaged or broken, or even with that pity that would come, so… "You know. Big brothers. They can get overprotective."

Something shifted in his eyes and he nodded. "Yeah." Then he laid his head back and closed his eyes.

"You're not sleeping on me, are you, Crispy?"

He grunted. "Keep it up and I'll find *you* a nickname."

"Anything to keep you awake."

"I'm just…watching the stars behind my eyelids."

"Fine. I'm going to make you a steak."

"Try not to set the house on fire."

"Hey. Firefighter in the house." She got up, but he

didn't open his eyes. Still, he looked better, less pale, his breathing steady. "How's the head?"

"Less banging. Can you find me a couple aspirin? Bathroom, above the sink."

She flicked on the light, the shadows of the late afternoon turning the cabin dusky. The air still smelled of his soap from his shower and, for a second, flashed the memory of him sitting on the floor. Frustrated, a little wrung out.

Clearly, Crispin didn't go down easily. And maybe she got that too.

The mirrored cabinet held a worn three-by-five snapshot of a young girl, maybe twelve, her hair in pigtails, grinning into the camera in front of what looked like a giant panda cage. She held up two fingers in a peace sign.

Jade found some ibuprofen and brought it out to him with water.

His breathing raked out hard from his broken body. She pressed her hand to his forehead—cool, no fever—and then picked up his wrist. Strong hands, bruised knuckles, which said he hadn't gone down easily. And his pulse had slowed, turned stronger. So maybe she'd let him sleep.

She cleaned up the broken glass from the window, dumped it into a trash bin, then looked for cardboard in his office. Nothing, but he did have a map on the wall similar to the fire map in the Jude County office. Dry erase markers circled areas on the map with tight, block handwriting with numbers and initials beside arrows to each circle.

And on his desk, a printout of pictures—some mug shots, others simply candids. He'd written names on many of them, the name *Floyd* noted on one with a bearded man, long hair, eyes of darkness. He'd added a couple exclamation points to the name.

No cardboard.

She went into the kitchen and pulled the steak from the bowl of water, where it was thawing. A cast-iron skillet sat on the stove along with a glass jar of bacon grease.

The steak sizzled and popped, and she seasoned it with salt, covered it, then went into the office to call Conner.

No answer.

So maybe the fire had gone from a surface fire to a crown fire, or worse. She stepped out and found the steak smoking—so yes, no fires today—and flipped it. Her stomach growled.

It felt all so…provincial. Like she'd stepped into a life she'd only ever seen from a distance. Not that she hadn't made a steak before, but…

Stop. She'd never gone down this road before for a reason. This was a weird nightingale moment, not a *date*. For crying in the soup, she didn't even know this man. So she should shut down the crazy warmth that stirred up inside her when he smiled at her.

What-*ever*.

She checked the steak, turned off the heat, and transferred it onto a plate to sit. Then she put a cover over it and walked back over to check on Crispin.

He roused, opened his eyes. Startled for a second when he saw her—it rippled through him in a quick breath, the tensing of his body. Then, "Oh. You."

You. Like she…what, belonged here? To make it worse, he sighed and smiled.

He possessed a devastating smile when he wanted to wield it.

"Steak's ready," she managed, but her voice came out weirdly high. Oh brother.

Then suddenly, lights flashed through the broken window, and a truck rolled into the driveway.

Crispin hit his feet as if he'd never gone down. Grabbed her hand and yanked her behind him.

She let him, the memory of shooting flushing through her.

He grabbed his AR-15 from the sofa. Only then did she realize he'd been sleeping with it.

The truck stopped and the front door opened. A man stepped out.

Crispin raised the gun —

"No. Stop. That's Conner, my boss. He's here to get me." She shoved the gun down and then headed for the door.

She nearly ran out of the cabin, down the steps toward Conner.

Conner wore his uniform and a JCFS hat, and came toward the deck eyeing the broken window. "You okay, Jade?"

Funny, she'd forgotten about her limp. "Yeah."

He gestured to the window. Oh, that.

"It's a long story. But I have a wounded man inside." Okay, that sounded a little, weirdly, possessive. "I found him at the source of the fire." Still sounded like she'd picked up a puppy or something. "There is a wounded man inside that needs medical assistance."

She headed back up the steps, across the porch, and opened the door.

No Crispin.

He wasn't standing in the dusky light of the family room, armed.

47

Nor in the bathroom. Or his bedroom, or even his office.

Where—

She came back out into the kitchen.

That's when she spotted the door, tucked away from the kitchen, in what she thought might be the pantry. "Crispin?"

She headed to the door, opened it.

The back door hung slightly ajar. What—

She opened it and stood on the small stoop, staring out at the tangle of forest.

"Crispin!"

The twilight ate her voice.

"Where'd he go?" Conner stood in the kitchen, staring out the window over the sink, then at her.

She shook her head. "I don't know."

Her gaze fell on the steak plate. The *empty* steak plate.

And despite the fist in her gut, she couldn't help but smile.

FOUR

Twenty-four hours of knocking down a fire, and Jade needed a cheeseburger.

A cheeseburger and maybe answers, although the second didn't seem anywhere in view.

Crispin had vanished. Simply ghosted into the wilderness.

And why not? Because after her statement to the local sheriff, a man named Hutchinson, about the attack at Crispin's cabin by The Brothers, she couldn't help but sense that maybe they thought *Crispin* might be the bad guy.

The sheriff had retrieved the bodies and declared the area a crime scene, but no one seemed at all worried that maybe, just maybe, Crispin might be in trouble.

Conner had no idea who he might be, and she got nothing from Miles either after she'd described him.

Frankly, deep in her gut she just felt...well, maybe Crispin needed to disappear.

But what if disappearing meant he landed right in another ambush of The Brothers?

"You okay?"

The question came from her pilot, Aria, who sat down next to her at the counter of the Hotline Bar and Grill, carrying a foamy chocolate milk and a basket of fries. She pushed the fries toward Jade.

Jade picked one out of the basket. "Yes. Just tired."

Aria nodded, also grabbing a fry. She dipped it into her milk, then popped it in her mouth. "That's what happens when you fight a fire for twenty-four hours without sleeping. But you got it knocked down, so bam." She held up a fist.

Jade met it. "The water dumps helped."

"Teamwork," said Aria. "The guys asked me if you want to join them at the pool table." She nodded across the room filled with smokejumpers and hotshots seated at tables and in the booths along the wall. At the pool table in the front, Vince and Finn had cued up, were shooting a round of eight ball.

At high tops, watching, sat Booth and Nova, clearly together by their animated conversation, the laughter. Booth wore a bit of desire in his eyes.

Jade couldn't remember a man ever looking at her that way.

Except—

No. That hadn't been desire from Crispin. It'd been a headache, and she'd held the cool cloth that'd soothed it. So, there. Big difference.

She'd met a few of the hotshots: Kane, Mack, and Ham—the Trouble Boys, as Aria had called them. And maybe they were, given the way they sat, surveying the room, back in their seats, definitely bearing an aura of military. They sat with JoJo Butcher and another female hotshot, Sanchez. Charlie, one of the older 'shots, ate fries in a booth with Orion, a good-looking guy in his early twenties.

Jade's burger arrived in a plastic basket, and Aria gestured to the pool table area. "C'mon."

Why not?

She walked over to an empty high top and sat down on a stool. Finn had banked a three ball into the corner pocket.

Aria took the other seat. "So, not a bad first couple days."

Jade glanced at her while she opened the top of the burger and added ketchup. "You mean no one got hurt?"

"That and you knocked down your first fire." She gestured to Orion. "Word on base is that he applied to be a smokejumper. You're one man—or rather, woman—down while Nova heals." Thankfully, her other injured smokejumper, Rico, had been given the all clear to join them on the next deployment.

"I got his application. It's not really up to me— Conner is at the helm of new recruits—but it's so late in the season. He needs to go through proper training. Better to bring in another 'shot from Alaska, or Missoula."

"Like your brother?" Aria pointed to a picture that hung on the wall of Jed and his legendary team. One of many, and of course, his picture hung beside years and years of other hotshot teams in this fire town.

On the other side of Jed's team picture hung the memorial picture of his mentor, Jock Burns, along with the other firefighters who had died in a terrible flashover accident a number of years back.

Jade took a bite of her burger, set it down and

wiped her mouth. "I hope not. First—he's boss of all the 'shots there. Second, I can't think of a worse nightmare than working for my brother." She sighed. "Let's just say he hates that I'm a smokejumper."

Aria raised a brow.

"When Jock and his team died, he called me. I was at Washington State University getting my undergrad in fire science, and he...well, let's just say that it was mostly panic and grief, and yeah, love, but...he said things I'm trying to forget. I hung up on him. We haven't spoken much since."

She took a sip of her soda. "I'm not sticking around. This is a short-term gig. Montana is just one state too close to Jed."

"Ouch," said Aria.

Vince scratched, and Finn pulled out his ball and set up for a new shot.

Jade nodded toward Booth and Nova. "So, what's with those two?"

"Oh. You know, fire romance. Booth saved Nova's life. Or maybe she saved his. He's sort of a mystery. Fun guy—likes to tell stories. Nova's had a thing for him all summer, although she wouldn't admit it. Glad to see it finally flashed over." She picked up a fry and winked. "He's a tough guy too, though. Chased down the arsonist who torched our HQ."

Jade had taken another bite and now put down her sandwich. "Really."

"Yeah. Finn saw him fight—said he looked like he might be ex-military."

Interesting.

Sounded a lot like a guy she knew.

And it could be a long shot, but...She slid off her stool.

Booth picked right then to head toward the bar, holding two empty glasses.

She caught up to him. "Hey. Can I talk to you?"

He looked down at her. Handsome guy, nearly as tall as Crispin, with long, dark-blond hair, a bit of a beard, and a wide set to his shoulders. Had a sort of swagger about him. "Sure, Chief. 'Sup?"

She glanced around, not sure why, then, "Do you know a guy named Crispin?"

He stilled, drew in a breath. "Who's asking?"

A terrible burst of hope filled her. "Me. I'm asking. I found him in a car wreck and took him back to his cabin, and then these guys shot at us, and he was wounded, and then when Conner showed up, he took off and—"

"Whoa." He set the glasses on the counter, then took her arm and motioned her outside. They stepped through the doors, the noise of the bar dying, and Booth walked her right over to the edge of the building, away from the door, into the shadows.

"You're sort of freaking me out."

"You're freaking *me* out," Booth said. "What do you mean Crispin was in a car crash? He's supposed to be in the *hospital*." He ran a hand across his forehead, shook his head. "I knew—I just knew he'd pull something like this. As soon as I gave him that phone..." He blew out a breath, then turned to her. "When was this?"

"Yesterday. Right after we jumped into the Rainbow Lake fire."

He nodded. "Right. Okay. And you say he was hurt? Beyond shot and beat up?"

She raised an eyebrow. "Um, he added a scratch to his leg, and I don't know—exposure, maybe. I

53

thought he might be going into shock, and he had a wicked headache—"

"He's giving me a wicked headache. But yeah, that sounds like Crispin. I guess I didn't really expect him to stay put. Not with The Brothers hunting him."

"Hunting him?"

He nodded. "They have assassins, hired to take him out."

She stilled. No wonder they'd found him at the house. But, "Who *is* Crispin? He said he was...well, he intimated that he was a secret agent or something."

Booth laughed then, something of humor, maybe chagrin. "Yeah. Or something." He looked at her, his smile dying. "Crispin is a patriot. And he's given a lot —too much—for his country. He was thought dead for a long, long time and probably would like to keep it that way, if you get me."

Oh.

"He's on a mission, and it's important. But here's what I know about Crispin." He leaned in, his gaze on hers. "He's just about the best guy I know. Tough and smart, and most of all, the guy who will get the job done, no matter what it costs." He sighed. "Do you know where he is now?"

"No. He took off like, poof, Casper the Ghost when Conner showed up."

"Figures." He nodded. "I hope he's all right."

Her too.

"Thanks for telling me," Booth said. "Please don't tell anyone else."

Gulp.

She nodded though, because henceforth, her lips were sealed. Booth headed back inside, but her appetite had died. As had her desire for camaraderie.

She walked out to Jed's bike, the one he still kept at his house just outside Ember.

She fixed on the helmet, got on the bike, and headed home. But Crispin followed her home, his words in her head. *You should leave me.*

No. See, that was just it. Try as she might, she couldn't tear herself away from his memory.

Jed's place sat on tiny Ember Lake, just north of town. A chalet-style home with a loft and a lower bedroom for their son. The deck overlooked the lake, the inside an open plan with a kitchen and great room, a two-story fireplace. During the winters, Jed worked on various facelift projects. She wondered if big bro knew she was here, bunking. Conner had told her that Jed had wanted it house-sat this summer while he was in Missoula.

So yeah, she felt a little like an interloper. Still, she couldn't remember having so much room to herself.

Now, she parked the bike in front of the house, took off the helmet, and went inside. The night had settled into the room, the moon glistening on the waters beyond the sliding glass doors and the deck.

She was reaching for the light when she saw him. A man, standing by the fireplace. Just standing, hands in his pockets, watching her. Her heart jerked, stilled.

Then her breaths came hard as he said, "And here I thought I lived dangerously."

She flicked on the light. Swallowed.

Crispin blinked, reopened his eyes. And smiled.

"Crispin!"

Don't hug him. Don't —

Nope. She took two steps toward him and

couldn't stop herself. She threw her arms around him, pulled him tight to herself. "You scared me."

He hesitated, then put his arms around her too, and weirdly, a sigh ushered out of him, deep and unhindered. "Yeah, well, that makes two of us." Letting her go, he met her eyes. "Seriously? A motorcycle?"

She paused, smiled, and then, aw, she started to laugh. "And here I thought you might be dead. When in fact, you're just annoying."

"Annoying?"

Not what Crispin had expected out of her mouth, but then again, he could never predict anything from her.

Like the *hug*? And he'd simply reacted, his mind blank, instinct taking over, causing him to lean in.

Hold on.

As if she might be the solid rock in the shifting waters of his crazy life.

She smelled good too, as if she'd showered. She wore leggings that did a great job of showing off what those canvas fire pants hadn't, and a T-shirt under the jean jacket. Her blonde hair fell onto her shoulders, shiny, and the entire ensemble made her look painfully, beautifully female.

He blew out a breath and stepped back a little, just in case he did something crazy and reached for her again.

What. *Ever.*

"Yes, *annoying*," she said. "Seriously—I jump from

airplanes into fire for a living, and you're worried about me riding a *motorcycle*?"

He ran a hand around the back of his neck.

"And that's a little pottish, isn't it? I mean, you're some secret agent being hunted by assassins, and *I'm* the one living dangerously?"

He stilled. Raised an eyebrow. "How did you know..." Oh no, he hadn't said something stupid during his feverish state on the sofa, had he?

"I had a little chatty-chat with your friend Booth."

Oh. He cleared his throat. "I, uh—"

"Save it, Tough Guy. I know you're on a *mission*. And..." She stepped up to him, her voice soft. "I know you were dead for three years."

He'd have to kill Booth. Slowly. "That's all classified. Or it was, until my sister was threatened and I ended up under a canoe with a bunch of campers and then in the hospital...okay, maybe it doesn't matter anymore."

"It matters to me. Why were you dead?"

"I didn't come here for this." He brushed past her, his heart a fist in his chest. First the hug, now the... the...He rounded on her. "I told you—you should stay away from me. People get killed around me." He held up a hand. "No more hugs."

She had turned on a lamp and now rolled her eyes. "We're past that. I taped up your gunshot. Sat by your bedside. Made you *steak*."

"Good steak, by the way."

"We're friends, like it or not, which means when you slink out in the middle of the night—"

"It was seven p.m.—"

"—and then show up in my living room at midnight—"

"It's ten."

" —scaring the stuffing out of me and then acting all worried about me—"

"I *was* worried."

"See. Then I get to hug you."

Oh.

"Don't let it go to your head, though. That was a friend's hug. *Friends*. It's a term people use when they share things with each other, like why they were dead for three years."

He took a breath. "I was double-crossed." He sighed. "Actually, the CIA was double-crossed. By a man named Alan Martin. He was working with a rogue faction inside the company. We knew there was a mole, and my boss set up a sting. What we didn't know was that the faction was onto us—Martin had gotten wind of the sting, and they ambushed us. Agents were killed, a bomb went off, and I was injured. I was also the last one standing. My boss got me to a secure facility and then told everyone I'd died."

He sat down, suddenly tired. "He did it to save my life. But it cost Booth his life too. He was my partner, and at the time of the bombing, he was in the hospital, taking care of his mom, who had some heart surgery or something. But the faction pinned the entire event on him, fingered him as the mole, and without my boss's quick thinking, he'd be in some CIA black site right now, without fingernails."

She didn't smile. Maybe she thought he was kidding.

"Henry sent him here, to Ember, where he's been working as a smokejumper for the last few years."

"And you?" Still the soft tone.

"I...mended. And then I got angry. I had a sister and a life and I didn't deserve to die. So I sent my sister a postcard, secretly, to tell her I was alive...just a hidden message, but she got it. And then I erased the old me and became Crispin Lamb, a name my sister gave me when we were kids." He got up, went to the kitchen. "I need water."

"Glasses are in the cabinet next to the sink."

He took one, filled the glass. Drank it. He hadn't realized how parched he was. But twenty-four hours hiking to one of his stashes, grabbing his truck, kitting up, and then tracking down Jade had worn him thin.

He needed about twelve hours of good sleep that wasn't in the back of an F-150.

"What has Crispin Lamb been doing for the past three years?"

He hadn't heard her get up, walk into the kitchen —hadn't expect her to be standing behind him, leaning against the counter. So close he could step up to her. Lean in.

Hold on.

He drew in a breath. Shook his head. "Tracking down the rogue agents, one by one."

She froze.

"The whole thing came out a few years ago. The CIA found out that the faction had been working with the Russians to cause all sorts of terror, from attempts on the president, to biological weapons, to staging attacks in other countries with the hopes of drawing America into a war. The faction was dissolved and Martin arrested—although he escaped prison, last I heard." He set the cup down. "The ones I didn't find went to prison. So I turned my attention to their partners."

"The Russians?"

"And specifically, The Brothers."

"Yes, the assassins in the woods."

"Mm-hmm." He sighed, then met her eyes. Still so beautiful, even in the dim light. "I'm sorry I got you involved in this."

"If memory serves, I'm the one who rescued you from your little tin-can car."

"It wasn't mine." He offered a wry smile.

"Oh brother."

"Still," he said. "This is where you need to forget you ever met me. Where we pretend we're not friends. And if anyone ever asks about me, you say, Crispin who?"

Her mouth opened. Closed. She shook her head.

"Jade—"

"Crispin. You can't…you need…"

"I can, and I don't need." He drew in a breath. "Please. The last thing I *do* need is to worry about you getting hurt."

Something shifted in her eyes then, and her mouth hardened. "Right."

He'd hurt her. "Jade."

"Why are you here then, Crisp?" Her tone matched the chill in her eyes.

Probably for the best. "I need my phone."

She just stared at him. Silence.

"You have it."

"I don't have it."

"Yes. You put it in your leg pocket. Back at the car."

Her mouth slowly opened. "Right. I forgot."

"Me too. All the way until today, when I realized there is information on it that I need. So...I tracked you down."

Her mouth made a tight line. "So, you weren't worried that I was worried."

He frowned, gave her a look. "Were you worried?"

"Of course I was worried! You were—are—hurt!"

"I'm fine."

"For the love. You were shot. Nearly went into shock. What, did you turn into Wolverine?"

A beat.

"Oh please. Don't tell me you don't know X-Men. Wolverine? Can heal himself?"

Oh. He smiled at that. "No. I mean...I just...it's mind over matter." But really, what would it hurt? "Fine. Yes. I'm tired. And sore—really sore. And living on the edge of ibuprofen, but..."

"But you have to finish the mission."

"Yes."

"Alone."

"Yes."

"Now you're *really* annoying me."

He drew in a breath. "Yes. Phone, please?"

She narrowed her eyes, then strode off to a nearby bedroom, slapping on the light as she went.

He waited in the kitchen. Took another drink. Resisted the urge to raid the fridge.

She returned, grabbed his hand, and slapped the phone into it. "It's probably dead."

Oh, right.

She stared up at him. "I'll make you a deal. I'll charge the phone, and you lie on that sofa and close your eyes for one whole hour. Maybe two. And then

61

I'll make you something to eat—I hope you like eggs —and let you walk out that door. Alone. I'll even give you a little wave."

He considered her, the way she stood, her hands on her hips, nearly glaring at him. "You are...bossy."

"We've been over this. No, I'm right. Take a load off, pal." She held out her hand. "Phone me."

He put the phone in her palm. She opened up a drawer and fished through it until she found the right cable. Then she plugged it into the wall.

"To the sofa, Rambo." She pointed.

He found himself obeying.

Toeing off his shoes. Lying on the sofa, his head on a pillow.

He closed his eyes to her putting a blanket over him.

And then, by George, he found exactly what he'd come here to really find but had been afraid to hope for.

Rest.

FIVE

And that was clearly that.

Jade leaned over the fire map in the command center of the fire station, trying, oh, trying to listen to Miles outline the latest fires spotted during this morning's drone flight.

"The Rainbow Lake fire jumped the Flatiron River here, twenty miles north of where you culled the front line, at the river's narrowest spot. It's now chewing its way north and west, to Canada, and down toward the main fire, still simmering its way south. These two heads meet and we'll have a real flare-up."

Flare-up. Like the crazy flash of emotions last night when she'd practically thrown herself into Crispin's arms?

Or maybe in the wee hours of this morning—he'd slept way, blissfully, past her one-hour terms—when he'd gulped down the plate of eggs she'd scrambled for him and drained a pot of coffee. Then he'd looked at her with those hazel-green eyes, his countenance, despite the fading bruises, seeming almost revived and said, "I think you might have saved my life."

"Me and every other short-order cook across

America, saving lives every morning." But his words had still done a number on her, finding footing in her heart.

He'd smiled then, and shoot, every time he did, it was only more lethal. Probably a good thing that he'd gotten up then, grabbed his charged phone, and walked to the door.

And probably *not* a good thing that she'd followed him and stood there, holding the door open, not sure what to say as he, too, stood there, looking down at her.

One step. That's all she'd needed to close the gap and really ignite something. She could almost feel his arms around her, almost taste his mouth on hers, and maybe he'd sensed it too, because he'd swallowed, cleared his throat, and said, "Take care of yourself," right before he'd practically fled out the door.

You too.

"So I think if you bring your team in here, Jade, you can use Pipe Creek as a break." He ran his finger along a creek spur, toward Tom Mountain. "There are a few homes in there, so make sure people have evacuated too."

She nodded, stifled a yawn.

"You good to go?" This from Conner.

"Yes," she said. "No one dies today." She gave him a thumbs-up, then headed out of the office, back to the gear area.

She then grabbed her chute pack, pulled out her chute and, on the long folding table, repacked it. No more tangles, thank you.

Booth came walking in, holding a cup of coffee. "Morning, Chief."

She glanced at him and looked away, and oh, she

hated holding secrets in her head, because in the forefront of her brain sat Crispin's story of Booth's secret identity, and now she wondered whether Nova knew, and maybe she should tell him that Crispin had visited her last night, and —

"Boss says the wind is all kinds of crazy today." He was packing his gear from the supplies in bins around the room.

"Mm-hmm."

Finn and Vince came in and opened their lockers. "Anytime you want to pay me," Finn said, probably to Vince.

Aria came in and set a duffel on the bench. "Hey, Jade," she said. "You didn't stick around last night."

"Sorry. Tired." And she stifled another yawn.

Booth glanced at her, frowned. "Something keep you up late?"

"I watched a reality show about singer Oaken Fox joining a SAR team in Alaska."

"I saw that," JoJo said. Jade hadn't seen her come in. "Did you get to the part where they have to search for the lost bridesmaids in a blizzard?"

Jade shook her head. Frankly, if she had, she might not even remember, because she'd dozed off in her brother's leather recliner, her earbuds still playing the show on her phone. But she hadn't wanted to take the chance of Crispin sneaking out on her again.

Take care of yourself. The words felt so...well, like he might be saying goodbye.

As in, not coming back.

Stop pining. Clearly, being around the man had her acting all sorts of crazy. She didn't like tough guys, didn't have room for romance, not with her short-term schedule in Montana. And moreover, well…she couldn't get in over her head, could she?

So she had no business flirting with the guy. Or standing at the door, hoping he'd kiss her.

She picked up her chute pack, her jump bag, and went to her locker. Grabbed her jumpsuit and stepped into it.

Layers. They protected her. Made her stronger. And maybe that's what had made Crispin both alluring and dangerous. She'd let him in, just a little.

But even a little could get her burned.

So yes, *take care of yourself*.

Putting on her boots and grabbing her helmet, she headed out to the plane. Aria walked around it, working her preflight check. Inside, Duncan had loaded the gear box and now checked the safety lines as the team loaded in and clipped them on. She got in, clipped her line to her carabiner, and took her spot on the first stick, alongside JoJo. Logan would jump last with Rico.

"Stay alert. Stay safe. No mistakes," she said as Duncan closed the door.

Then she sat back, her eyes closed, and absorbed the rumble of the Twin Otter as it took off and soared over Ember, toward their jump site.

Mind on the jump. On the fire. On the team.

She must have dozed off, because Duncan nudged her knee when they reached the jump site. Crawling over to the open door, she followed the trail of the spotter ribbon down to the ground. Below them, the fire had just started to crown the trees, and she identified the creek where they could cut the line and start a backfire.

"Your jump site is over there, in that clearing!"

Duncan shouted, and she guesstimated it might be a good two miles from the creek. But, with the dense forest, the safest place to land.

Aria descended, then circled, and Duncan pushed out the gear box.

Jade signaled to JoJo, who gave her a thumbs-up. They went out the door.

Wind, brisk and holding just a nip of chill from the morning. She counted her thousands, then pulled, and her toggles came out unhindered. JoJo's chute deployed without a hitch, and by the time Jade had landed—a perfect land, roll, and look—the rest of the team were floating down.

No mistakes.

She gathered up her chute, packed it away, then shed her jumpsuit and replaced the gear in the box— saws and shovels and water bottles—with the packed chutes and suits.

The smoke rose from the fire line, billowing into the clear blue sky, some two klicks away, around the mountain and through the woods.

She'd spotted an old forest road on her descent, so she aimed for that, leading the team through the rocky terrain toward the scrape in the earth.

As they walked, the air grew denser, although still clear of the smoke, just a hint of odor burning the air. Behind her, Vince, Rico, and Finn barely grunted with their gear, and JoJo and Logan took up the rear.

"Hey," Booth said. "Anyone want to hear a story?"

She glanced over her shoulder. "What?"

"He does this," JoJo shouted. "He loves his tall tales."

"Not a tall tale," he said. "This one is about this guy I know—"

"Wait! Is his name Henry?" Vince said.

Laughter. She frowned, looked again at Booth. He shrugged. "It's a thing."

Some guys sang songs, others told stories, a few others simply kept quiet, the stories of fire in their eyes. So she got it.

"Save it for tonight," she said, stopping and pulling out her topo map from her pants pocket. "There should be a homestead around here. Let's make sure it's evacuated, and then we'll hit the creek, due south."

Booth looked over her shoulder along with Logan. They nodded.

She shouldered her Pulaski and headed toward the drive to the homestead. An indentation in the woods, really, about as wide as a pickup, but recent tire tracks had churned up dirt, so maybe the inhabitants had left. The forest had thickened, shaggy blue spruce and tall white pine crowding against willow and poplar scrub on either side of the narrow road.

Sweat trickled down the back of her shirt, and her ankle had started to protest, but not enough to slow down.

They did this right, she'd end the night with a basket of fries at the Hotline—

A gunshot. It exploded into the air and she froze.

"Was that—"

"Get down!" The voice came from the woods, unseen, but—

Her knees buckled, and she landed on all fours. What—

She looked back to check out her team. Logan had pushed JoJo down, his hand over her pack, his other arm above his head. Vince and Finn both dropped their saws, and Rico dove for the ditch.

Booth, next to her, crouched, his pack shed and —

"You have a gun?"

"It's a bear gun, and yes."

"Bears?"

"Reasons —"

Another shot, and this time a tree shook nearby.

"Is someone shooting at us?" This from JoJo, who started crawling for the ditch, her hands over her head. Logan followed her.

"Get off the road!" The voice echoed from the brush.

Jade searched for the voice, her heart a fist in her ribs. What —

And then, just like that, he burst out of the woods. He wore black camo pants, a black jacket, his face grimy, and she'd recognize him anywhere.

Tough Guy.

He held a shotgun in one hand.

Crispin's gaze landed on Booth, then on Jade right before he grabbed her pack and hauled her up. "To the woods!"

She scrambled with him, nearly falling as he hauled her off the road, practically threw her into the trees. "Hide!"

Hide?

JoJo and Logan dove into the woods, Rico still in the ditch, along with Finn now.

Vince and Booth, however, simply made themselves small and headed for trees on the opposite side.

Another shot, and this one stripped off bark over Vince's head.

That's when she spotted a gun in Vince's hand too. What, was her whole team armed?

But—"Crispin. What are you—"

"Just stay down, Jade." He pressed on her shoulder and didn't look at her, just studied the road.

Her heart stopped cold as a truck appeared, motoring down the narrow path, two men standing in the back like real-life terrorists, their semiautomatics sweeping the road.

"Don't. Move," Crispin whispered.

She couldn't breathe, so no problem.

But—"What is going on? Are you following me?"

He shot her a look, a fierceness in it, and then, "No, I'm not following you. Are you following me? Because you just managed to walk right into a Brothers camp."

And then, as if she might be an extra in an episode of *Seal Team*, she crouched in the ditch and watched as Crispin, Booth, and even Vince jumped up, secured behind the trees, and fired back.

"What are you doing?"

"What do you think I'm doing? Stay down!" He glanced at her.

A bullet chipped the tree near his shoulder.

"I'm down, I'm down!" She made herself very, very small and prayed no one died today.

Hours later, the image of Jade crouching in the woods, bullets shredding the trees around her, could still shake Crispin through to his bones.

If he hadn't been there—

He stood now, outside the ring of firelight from

the team's strike camp, watching—yes, turning into a voyeur, maybe—as Jade and the rest of the team set up tents, the darkness settling around them.

They'd left a trail as wide as a bulldozer through the woods, so he'd tracked them down easily after canvassing the small cabin where the three Brothers gang members had holed up.

Maybe he shouldn't be here, but he needed to update Booth on what he'd found. The picture sat folded in the pocket of his cargo pants. A bit of providence he'd found inside the house, tacked to a wall, along with a topo map, locations circled.

He recognized the locations as other Brothers camps he'd found. Floyd Blackwell's various hideouts.

Providence had been on his side this time, given the fact he'd spotted the smokejumper team just as they'd strolled into Brothers territory. What if—

No. This time, he'd been there. And with Booth. He didn't know the other jumpers, but between the three of them—himself, Booth and the other armed jumper—they'd managed to wound one of the targets before the truck had driven down the road, screaming up dust.

He'd searched the cabin while the team had deployed to the site, and maybe for the best, because in his head, he rounded back to Jade and—

What? Pulled her into his arms to try and still the shaking inside? Demand she not do her job? Smokejumpers walked into trouble all the time...

He blew out a breath, watching her now. She seemed tired—sooty, grimy, a day of working on the line showing in her movements. But they wouldn't have hiked out and set up a strike camp if the fire still threatened.

His foot cracked a branch, and he stilled as Booth looked up, toward the shadows. Reached for his weapon—and no wonder. Poor man lived in two worlds now that Crispin had made the mistake of coming back from the dead.

Putting out his hands, he stepped out of hiding. "Booth. It's me."

Booth wore the day's exertion on his sooty face, his yellow Nomex jacket blackened, his hair matted from his helmet. He lowered the gun. "Crisp. What are you doing here?"

Others on the team had looked up. Vince, a guy who clearly had some military or law enforcement past, the way he'd instinctively taken cover, then aligned with them to protect the team. And another woman who crouched in front of the stove, boiling water, probably for dinner. The team had circled the tents with clotheslines strung between them, a few washed bandannas hanging from the lines, along with socks. Jackets also hung from the lines, a few of the team having shed their outer layer.

He glanced at Jade, who'd stilled, lowering the radio. He'd heard her checking in with HQ as he stood in the shadows. No pickup until morning.

Now, "I just, um…wanted to see if you'd had any more trouble."

"Just a fire trying to kill us," Jade said. "Hungry?"

"I don't want to—"

"Booth, you have room for him in your tent?" Jade asked.

Booth shrugged. "I'll have to kick Logan out, but he snores, so—"

"Seriously, it's the smoke. I don't snore—"

Booth smiled and Logan shook his head.

"Gimme your MREs," the woman at the fire said. "Water's boiling."

"Here you go, Jo," said Booth, walking over to his pack. He glanced at Crispin. "Chicken à la King."

"Yum."

"I have an extra," Jade said and set two metallic packets beside the others. Jo filled them with water.

Booth motioned him over with a gesture of his head. Lowered his voice. "How was it that you happened to be right there to save our hides?" He bent in front of his tent, opened it, then grabbed a nearby sleeping bag and tossed it inside.

"The short of it is that I stopped by the sheriff's office today."

"Bold move, since you ditched his deputy."

"He had some choice words but seemed more concerned with the dead guys they found at my house —one had my picture on his body, so Sheriff Hutchinson thinks they might be the assassins you mentioned."

"I'd really love to stop looking over my shoulder."

"Soon, bro. But I still need to find Henry. Remember that pickup you stole to spring me from Floyd's cabin? The back glass was shot out?"

"You remember that?"

"I remember you dragging my sorry backside out of a burning cabin, yes. Anyway, when I was in town, I spotted the truck and followed it into the woods. I was staking out the place when you guys came trotting down the road."

"Floyd?"

"Nope. Not there."

Booth's mouth made a tight line as he nodded.

"Did you find anything when you searched the place?"

"Yep. A picture."

"Yours?"

"Nope."

"Please don't tell me it's mine."

"Nope." He pulled the photograph from his pocket. "Look familiar?"

The picture, taken from a distance, portrayed a man knee-deep in water, holding a throw-back fish on a fly rod. Narrow face, short white beard, his equally white hair framing a furrowed brow, pensive blue eyes.

"Crazy Henry."

"Living his best clandestine life in a *River Runs Through It* set, here in the backwoods of Montana."

"Did you get to those coordinates I gave you yet?"

"Yes. Early this morning before I hit up the sheriff. It's an abandoned cave." He shook his head. "So we're back at nothing."

Booth pointed at the picture. "Not nothing. He rescued my girlfriend, Nova—"

"Girlfriend?"

A wry grin crested across Booth's face. "Yeah, I'm trying that word out. I think I like it." Booth shrugged. "It's about time we escaped this nightmare." He stood up and headed to the stove, where his dinner waited.

The others sat, spoons in the bags of food, eating their rehydrated dinners. Jade picked up her MREs. "You have a choice of chili mac or beef stew."

"Stew," he said. "Are you sure?"

"Sure that you saved my life today, so yeah." She met his eyes as she handed him the pouch. Her voice fell. "I don't know what you were doing there — probably I don't want to, but…thanks."

He nodded. "You okay?" She'd washed her face and donned a clean black T-shirt, combed back her blonde hair, beauty from the ashes.

"Yeah. I think." She handed him a spoon, then sat down on a nearby rock and dug into her chili mac.

"You get the fire out?" He sat down next to her.

"We cut a line, set a burn, and yes, routed it back onto itself. HQ sent a drone over today, and it looks like it's dying, at least this spur. The 'shots are still fighting the blaze on the western side of the river."

"Headed for Snowhaven."

"Hopefully not." She blew on a spoonful of mac, ate it, then downed it with water. "Sorry I don't have another jug. But you can have some of mine."

He accepted it, handed it back. "Thanks."

They sat shoulder to shoulder on the rock, his leg against hers, the sense of it oddly intimate, like they might be partners.

Girlfriend. The word sneaked through him, attached.

What. *Ever.*

But then his memory flashed with her in his arms, the feel of her body against his, the smell of her and —

He got up. "Um. I — "

"That's it. You pop in, save my life, eat my food, and leave?"

His eyes widened.

"Sit back down, Tough Guy. I know you're still on a 'mission.'" She one-hand quoted the last word. "But frankly, I need answers. Like…how'd you know we were there?"

Oh. "Uh — "

"Wait. If you tell me, will you have to kill me?"

He gave her a look. She grinned, then patted the seat next to her.

He sat back down. Not enough room to scoot away, but...

Aw, shoot, why had he come here? Booth had the ability to protect her.

"Hey—you dropped something." She bent down and picked up the folded picture. Must have dropped from his pocket.

Her gaze stayed on the open picture, longer than a casual look. "I know this guy. This is Henry Snow." She looked at him. "Older, for sure. But this is near his cabin, up by Blue Mountain. He's looking very Ian McKellen with that white beard."

"What?"

She handed him the picture. "You know—Gandalf, and Magneto. Oh, wait, you don't know the X-Men." A sort of tongue-in-cheek disgust edged her tone.

"No—I mean, you know Henry?"

He glanced at Booth, who looked over, frowned. Then back to Jade.

"Sure. Sweet old guy, lives in the woods? He had a cabin maybe a mile or so from Wildlands Academy. We used to see him occasionally out with his dog, Bond. I don't know if he's still around."

"We're hoping he is," Crispin said, his heart thundering. He took a breath. "Can you...do you know how to find the cabin?"

"Sure. I mean, it's not on any road on the map, but I spotted it a couple times during the summer when we were out hiking. I think I could find it again."

He must have made a face.

"Wait…is this your *mission*?"

He sighed. "I need to find him. Talk to him."

She dropped her spoon into the pouch. "Done. I have a couple days off. When I get back to town, we can head up there."

Oh.

"You're wearing that look again, Tough Guy." She shook her head. "Listen. You're not going to find him without me. And frankly, you need a partner."

He glanced at Booth, who could clearly hear their conversation, one eyebrow up.

Partner.

"I don't need—"

"Yes, you do. Finish your stew. There's pudding where that came from." She got up.

Okay, he'd find Henry, secure the missile—would probably have to call in the big guns for that—and then bring her back to civilization before he tracked down Floyd and finished this.

And then what?

His gaze wandered back to Jade, to her adding water to a couple small packets of chocolate pudding, and her words from earlier today found him. *Are you following me?*

No. Yes. Maybe.

But weirdly, Crispin had stopped shaking.

And maybe providence was on his side after all.

SIX

Of course he'd ghosted her the next morning. Not that she'd expected any less from Crispin slash Bourne, but still, when she got up and spotted Booth alone, heating up water on the stove, she knew.

"He said he'll meet you at your place," Booth said quietly.

A haze of residual smoke hovered through the forest. Usually a fire died down during the night, and they were a good mile from the front. Still, she should probably check on the drone coverage this morning, along with their ride back to Ember.

She nodded at Booth's words and retrieved her dried handkerchief from the line. For now, she used it to tie back her tangled hair, now knotted in a hairband. Grime infiltrated her pores, soot embedded her cells, her bones. An hour under a cool shower might not be enough.

"You really know where Crazy Henry is?"

She came back to the fire, frowned. "He's not crazy."

Booth made a sound, deep in his throat.

"What?"

"Nothing. Just...watch your back."

She frowned again. "Why? Bad guys in the woods?"

"Maybe."

She'd been kidding, sorta. But maybe not, considering the last few days. "What do they want with Henry? He's a harmless old guy who likes to fish."

Another deep sound.

"Booth."

"Nope. But I'm sure you're right." The water boiled, and he poured it out into instant grounds. "Besides, you'll be with Crispin. He won't let anything happen to you."

"Have you taken a good look at your friend? He's still hurting."

"He's fine. He's Crispin." He took a sip of his coffee, then eyed her. "Wait. You *like* him."

"What? I mean—sure. He's...we're friends."

"Nope. Crispin doesn't have room for friends. Never has."

"Weren't you his partner or something?"

"A long time ago."

She retrieved a cup and added instant grounds, then poured herself a bracing stew.

"But he's always worked alone, really. I was sort of just Robin to his Batman."

"I'm sure you were more than that."

"I had to track him down and make him tell me about The Brothers. And that was after I was nearly killed. So...Crispin makes a point of not needing anyone."

"No one doesn't need anyone." Around her, tent doors had started to unzip.

He cut his voice down. "Crispin is a great guy. Like I said—a patriot. He always—*always*—does the right thing. But he's gotten used to relying on himself." He gave her a look. "Even if he did agree to your help this one time."

"What are you trying to say, Booth?" She, too, had lowered her voice.

JoJo had stepped out of the tent.

"I just don't want you to get burned."

She drew in a breath. "I've got thicker skin than you think. I'm practically fireproof. But don't worry —nothing is happening between us."

He raised an eyebrow, and she stepped away as JoJo came to the fire. "Mornin'."

"Morning," he echoed, his gaze on Jade.

She took another sip of coffee, then turned to JoJo. "I'll get eggs from the kit."

They'd tied up the food pack overnight, but now it lay on the ground, Booth having retrieved the coffee earlier. She found the powdered egg pouch, handed it to JoJo, then headed over to a clearing to call Conner.

No new fires overnight, and yes, he'd dispatched a bus to pick them up.

You like him. Booth's words sat in her head as she packed up her tent, then the gear box, and finally, with the team, hiked down to the service road to meet the crew bus, a twelve-passenger van.

No, she didn't *like* him. Except, her brain kept returning to his bursting from the forest, shouting *get down*, his hazel-green eyes on her, fierce, painfully protective.

The way he'd grabbed her, pulled her to safety.

Put his hand on her shoulder when he'd told her to stay put.

Even the fact he'd shown up last night... *Are you following me?*

Shoot, her stupid heart hoped so.

She stared out the window of the van, her jaw tight. Brilliant, Jade. Because suddenly she saw herself laughing with him, maybe letting him ride with her on her—Jed's—bike, and making them steaks, and hel-*lo, she was not staying in Montana*.

And he had a life here—or sort of, and...

Oh boy. Because what if she *did* stay? What if—

They pulled up to HQ, and she spotted a bulldozer tearing down the front of the burnt building, scraping the charred beams down to the earth to start over.

What if she...started over? Here, in Montana?

No. What—no. She had a life in Alaska. Besides, Jed's gig in Missoula would end in August, and she'd need to pack her bags. No room for two Ransoms in Ember.

So. Just partners, then. On the hunt for sweet old Henry.

They piled out, and she helped unpack the truck, then brought the gear to the ready room in the Quonset hut. Dragging out her jumpsuit from the gear box, she hung it in her locker, then brought her chute to the hanging room.

"Hey, Duncan." The spotter stood at a long table, checking chutes for damage.

"Another successful mission," he said and gave her a thumbs-up. "Good job, Ransom."

"Thanks. Hey, I got this tear in my jacket." She

shed it and put it on the table, showed him where the jacket had separated. "Can you sew it up?"

He frowned at her. "What happened?"

"Got hit by a branch."

He pointed to her shoulder. "You're bleeding."

She could barely see it. But the wound must have opened after she'd patched it up last night, quietly, in the darkness of her tent. "It's fine."

"You should get it checked out."

"Aw, it's nothing. Thanks for sewing up the coat."

She returned to her locker and pulled on her jean jacket before anyone could notice. It did smart, but not enough to slow her down.

And of course, it wasn't from a branch. But she didn't need questions. Or pity.

She'd unpacked and stowed her gear and was headed into the office to talk to Conner when Booth stopped her. "Crispin won't do it, so you make sure you call me if you need me."

She cocked her head. "It's just a ride into the woods to see an old friend."

"Yep," he said.

"Fine. Okay." Then she brushed past him, toward Conner's office.

"I already know about the shooting," Conner said as she came in. "But what I don't know is why you didn't call me right away." He pointed to a chair.

Oops. "Truth is, there wasn't time. We had to kick down the fire. But I'm here now. Still—how'd you find out?"

"Sheriff called, asked me to ask you to come by and give him a statement. Not sure how he knew."

She had a guess it started with a *C* and ended in *ispin*. "Will do."

He drew in a breath, then turned to the map on the wall. "I know you have two days off, but I can only give you twenty-four without being on call, just in case this fire gets out of hand. I have another jump team coming in, so you'll be the second team we call out, but we need you ready."

Oh. But Henry's place might only be an hour from here. She'd be back by tonight. "Aye, aye, boss."

He looked at her. Shook his head. "I don't know what it is about you, Jade, but nothing rattles you."

She smiled. No need to get rattled when you'd already faced the fires and survived. Instead, "Thank you, sir. I try." She got up.

"That Jed's bike out there?"

She raised an eyebrow. "Could be."

He shook his head, but a smile touched his mouth. "You like to live dangerously."

She laughed. "I'll have my phone with me."

But his words sat with her. Dangerously. No, no she didn't. Or not usually.

Jed's bike sat in the morning shade, and she donned her helmet, got on, and fired it up.

The air skimmed off a layer of grime as she drove home.

A hot shower skimmed off the rest. Not quite an hour, but she stayed under the spray a long time, letting the ambush and the fire and even Booth's words wash off her.

She didn't like Crispin. He wasn't her type— dangerous and moody and a loner. No, she didn't like him at all.

She just felt...sorry for him. Yes, that was it.

Getting out, she changed into a clean sports bra, a white short-sleeve T-shirt, and cargo pants, pulled on a flannel shirt, then braided her hair and added a bandanna.

Then she grabbed the small black ring off the dresser and slid it onto her ring finger, right hand.

She came out into the kitchen. Crispin sat on her deck, staring out at the lake, in one of Jed's Adirondack chairs. At least this time he hadn't broken in, but it gave her a moment to just consider him against Booth's words.

Crispin doesn't have room for friends. Never has.

Maybe not. Because he seemed like a lone wolf, with his beard, his dark hair, the solemn expression. He wore a pair of black combat pants, a lightweight gray long-sleeve shirt, and boots. And what looked like a knife attached to his belt.

Yet he held a cup of coffee in a paper cup, like just a guy, hanging out.

So maybe friends, at least for today.

Sliding open the door, she stepped out onto the deck. "Hey."

"Hey," he said and took a sip of coffee.

"So, what's the deal with Henry? Booth was tight-lipped."

"Mm-hmm."

"Nope." She sat on the arm of the other chair. "What's going on? And I don't care if you have to kill me."

He glanced over at her, no smile, but maybe a touch of humor in his eyes?

She offered a half smile.

He sighed and set his coffee on the arm of the chair. "Okay, so I mentioned that I was dead for three years."

"Yes."

"And that I was in the CIA."

"Hard to miss." She got up and moved the chair to face him and sat in it. "Go on."

"So, I left out the part about the sting being the sale of a nuke to the rogue CIA faction."

She stilled. "A real nuke."

"A missile, yes. A Phoenix missile—compact—ten feet tall and two feet wide, about six hundred pounds. A prototype, but functioning. It has a range of five hundred miles and can carry a low-yield nuclear warhead. It also has an advanced guidance system that can be remotely controlled and activated. The tricky part is the AI component that was built in."

"A missile that can think."

"Yes. Which means it can adjust to find the area where the blast can be most destructive in a given set of parameters."

"I'll never sleep again. Excuse me while I start prepping. Please tell me this is not the artwork of a bad player."

"Unless you include the US government."

"I might. Sometimes." She drew in a breath. "So, this faction wanted to get their hands on the missile and sell it? To whom?"

"The Russians."

"Oh, just them. Right. Because we're in a Bond movie."

He laughed, and shoot, the deep rumble of it simply went right through to her bones, her cells. Sparked a terrible longing that *no, no, no—just friends, Jade!*

But she could be his Robin, today.

"Okay, so how does Henry play into this?"

"Right. So Henry White—Snow—was my handler. And Booth's handler."

"Handler."

"As in—"

"I watched *Alias*."

"So, this wasn't quite *Alias*."

"True. You don't have Jennifer Garner's legs. Or skimpy outfits."

He looked at his legs, back to her. "Should I change?"

And now she laughed. "Did you just try and be funny?"

"You can't have all the fun."

"Okay, your handler, crazy old sweet Henry Snow-White—"

"Stole the nuke."

Words were stripped from her.

He took a sip of coffee.

"No, he didn't."

"He absolutely did. To protect it because we didn't know who the bad guys were. And then he hid it."

"In his garage?"

"I hope he found a better place than that."

She did too. "So, now what?"

"Now The Brothers are trying to find him before I do, grab the nuke, and sell it to Russia."

"Why are we sitting here?" She made to get up.

"Wait."

"What? Are you going to tell me the Chinese are after us too?"

"I hope not. But I am going to say this, and please hear me, because I'm only going to say it once."

She sat back, her eyes purposely wide.

His mouth tightened. Eyes narrowed. "You do everything I say. Stay with me—don't wander off—"

"I'm not the one who ghosts—"

He ignored her. "If I say run, you run. You don't look back. You don't try to help me. You run."

His gaze had turned nearly ferocious, his tone lethal. Ho-*kay*. She nodded. "You're a little scary."

"Good. Finally."

"And bossy."

"Otherwise known as right." He raised an eyebrow.

"Hardy har har." She got up. "Let's go."

He'd gotten up too but now caught her arm. "Jade, are you hurt?"

She froze.

"You're bleeding. On your shoulder." He took a step toward her.

She jerked away. "I'm fine." She turned, but he grabbed her hand.

"You're not fine. What's going on?"

No, no, no—"I got hit by a branch. It's no big deal. C'mon."

But he didn't move. And…that was just *it*. "I'm not as fragile as I look, Tough Guy. So do you want to stop World War Three or not?"

Then she turned her back to him and nearly fled the porch.

Crispin always felt like he possessed the emotional depth of a teaspoon, but even he could see that he'd done something to upset Jade.

She sat in the passenger side of the bench seat of

his vintage F-150, staring out the window, her jaw tight.

I'm not as fragile as I look, Tough Guy.

He couldn't scrape her words from his mind, and now, as they headed out of Ember, west to County 518—at her direction—they burned inside him. "I don't think you're fragile."

She looked over at him. "What?"

"Fragile. I don't think you're fragile. I think you're...well, you might be the toughest woman I've ever met. And that's saying something, because I've known more than a few female agents. None of whom would strap on a parachute and jump into a fire."

He glanced at her, but she just swallowed.

He didn't know why he cared, really. Maybe because, yes, this was all kinds of wrong, him taking her to find Henry, and if he were honest with himself...

Maybe it was better not to be honest. It wasn't like they had a future. They were barely friends. He'd call them...partners. For the day. Like...a female Booth. So, "Are you always this ornery?"

This got a response. One eyebrow shot up. "Ornery? That's rich, coming from Mr. Ornery himself. You cornered the market there, grumpy-pants."

Grumpy-pants? "I'm not grumpy. I'm serious. Focused."

"High scorer on Whac-A-Mole."

"What?"

"You know that game—"

"I know the game. I just...okay, so yes, I'm trying to keep life from exploding—literally, I might add—but...fine. Maybe I am wound a little tight. But..."

He turned onto the county road. "I wasn't always…" He sighed. Swallowed.

"There is a complete sentence in there. I know there is." She turned toward him.

And at least she had started to warm, so, okay, why not?

"I've sort of been on my own since I was eighteen and my parents were killed in an earthquake."

Silence.

Aw, probably he could work on his delivery, but he hadn't had much opportunity for practice, having tucked that super awesome event deep inside his chest for nearly fifteen years.

She put her hand on his arm, and he stiffened. But her hand tightened around his bicep, and he glanced at her.

"I just wanted you to know that I'm sorry. That's terrible." She released her hand, but the warmth stayed. And it helped ease the story out.

"It was Easter Sunday, 2010. We were living in a small town just north of Baja, California. My dad worked border control, my mom was a veterinarian. We had a little place outside town with horses. It was a ranch home, walkout style. The earthquake happened a number of miles away, and we barely felt it. What we didn't know was that it had cracked the center beam of the house—a very old house— and afterwards, they thought maybe it had already been broken. I was out with some buddies. We were just hanging out, playing video games at a friend's house, when the aftershock hit. I was in town, and we had decided to get midnight pizza when we heard sirens, and a bunch of the guys thought—let's go. Chase the ambulance, you know." He swallowed, his throat dry. "I followed them all the way to my house."

"Oh no."

"The house had caved in. My parents had a walkout basement master—it had been remodeled into a big suite. They loved it—it looked out to the mountains. My sister was upstairs in her bedroom. The house collapsed into the master suite. She could hear them shouting for her, but she couldn't get to them. I don't know how she lives with that memory, but…I can't get it out of my head."

She hadn't touched him again. And maybe that was good, because he hadn't really told anyone the story.

"I stood outside, watching the firefighters, and I lost it. I tried to get in—they had to cuff me and throw me in a cruiser. And then I just sat there and cried." He closed his mouth, and a terrible sound emerged from his chest. He cleared his throat. "Anyway, my sister survived, and she was thirteen, so I got custody. We lived on the life insurance for a while. Moved to Last Chance County, where I studied criminal justice at a local community college. When she turned eighteen, we moved to Nevada, and I finished my degree at Nevada State. Top of my class."

"No doubt."

"I got recruited by the three letter companies right out of school. I picked the CIA and sort of regretted it right away."

"Really?"

He looked at her. "I was young and eager, and I went undercover, and…let's just say that I was reckless. By this time my sister had moved to Idaho, and I wanted to play big brother and check in. I was working in Mexico, dismantling a cartel, and somehow brought the danger home. She had to change her name. She moved to Wyoming and then finally ended up here. Where…of course, I nearly got her killed again."

"I see."

He glanced at her. "What do you see?"

She cut her voice low, imitating him. "*You should leave me. Get away from here.*"

Oh.

"So yes, I get it. And suddenly, what Booth said about you makes sense."

So going to kill Booth. "What did he say?"

"He called you a lone wolf."

On the other hand, maybe Booth had done him a solid. Because then she wouldn't get her hopes—aw, see that's what lying to himself did. Because frankly, *he* was the one with hopes way out of control, somewhere in the outer atmosphere.

Rein it in, Tough Guy.

"Listen. I also get wanting to…go it alone." She had taken a breath. "But we weren't designed that way. God created us to be in community. You've heard that saying—it's not good for man to be alone?"

"That was about Adam."

"It was about man. Which I think, from all outward appearances, you are."

"I am."

"Thought so. So, pardner, stop being so grumpy. Everything happens for a reason. Go with it. Take a right up here." She pointed to a mile marker and then a dirt road.

He turned. The entire drive, smoked had cluttered

the sky to the east. But here, it seemed to darken, as if the fire might be closer.

Hopefully not overrunning Henry's place, because, hello—nuclear missile. But he wouldn't be so careless as to hide it in his, well, garage, right?

He sighed, looked at her. "I don't get you, Jade. You're always so...calm. Like Teflon."

"Why worry about things I can't control? I have today. And that's all I need to worry about."

He frowned.

"It's something my mother said to me when I was young. Just today. Survive today."

Interesting words. *Survive?*

"She used to ask me, 'Is it well with your soul?' And when she put it like that...it sort of focused everything. Because in the end, that's what matters, right? So I just...survive this day—oh my—" She sat up. "There's something on fire up there."

He slowed and peered through the woods. Flames curled around an outbuilding, sparks shooting into the sky.

A garage fire.

"That's Henry's house!" She pointed to a cabin about a hundred yards from the garage, not on fire— yet.

He slammed the gas down, gunned the truck over the rutted road, right into the yard. She had piled out before he threw the car into Park.

"Jade! Stop!"

But of course, just like he'd predicted, she didn't pause to obey him.

She landed on the front porch, then grabbed the door—

"Jade! Wait—what if there's—"

She disappeared inside.

—an assassin inside.

He grabbed his Browning 12 gauge from behind the front seat.

Then he followed her into the house, bracing himself.

Stopped.

She knelt on the floor next to an older man who was skinnier than Crispin remembered and bleeding from a head wound. A Glock 19 lay not far from his reach.

"Get me a towel!" Jade shouted.

He scanned the room first—all clear—then grabbed a towel from the counter. Tossed it to her.

She pressed it on the man's head. "It's okay, Henry. It's going to be okay."

The man groaned, and Crispin walked over to him.

Blood matted his whitened hair, and he must have been knocked out, because he woke with a rush, a jerk, and stared at Jade, grabbing her hand.

"Get away from me!"

She scrambled back, and that's when Crispin stepped over the man, crouched in front of Jade. "Henry. It's me—Cris—um—" Shoot. Maybe Henry wouldn't remember that name. "It's Ethan. Ethan Tucker."

Henry blinked at him, then pushed himself up. Glanced at Jade, then put his hand to his forehead, and his face began to buckle. His voice dropped, and he shook his head, his eyes on Crispin. "Oh, Ethan. Ethan—you're too late."

SEVEN

Yes, Jade heard what Henry had said about being too late.

Also heard Crispin's real name—Ethan. She liked it. He seemed like an Ethan.

But mostly, she spotted sparks landing on the porch of Henry's cabin, and her firefighter brain fixed on—house fire.

And then *conflagration*, if this thing took on new life.

"Get some ice on his wound. See if you can stop the bleeding," she said to Crispin—she couldn't wrap her brain around the *Ethan* quite yet.

He picked up Henry around the shoulders and helped him to a worn sofa. A stone chimney ran up one side of the cabin with a small living area, a rag rug on the floor, and a kitchen with a gas stove and a round table.

"You have a hose?" she asked Henry as she headed to the door. Sparks, carried by the wind, spat on the house and had already ignited spot fires in the dry grass.

"On the side of the house. From a well in the

yard," Henry said, his hand to the towel on his forehead.

"Shovel?"

"In the garage."

Not great.

"I might have one at the back of the house, in the garden."

In the kitchen, Crispin dumped ice onto a towel. "We need to get to the nuke."

"It's too late. Floyd and another guy were waiting for me. I managed to nick the other man, but they'd already ransacked my office—"

He pointed to a room on the far side of the cabin, the door ajar. A glimpse inside evidenced his words— papers on the floor, drawers upturned. "They grabbed the topo map—I'd marked the silo where Fanny sleeps. My plan was to give you the map when you arrived."

"Fanny?" Crispin came over with the towel.

"The Phoenix missile." He held the towel to his head. "They stole my truck—I tried to stop them and hit the propane tank." He took the towel. "They're about twenty minutes ahead of us."

"We need—"

"We need to stop that fire before it spreads to the house and the surrounding forest," Jade said, and ran outside.

The garden hose lay coiled in the back, already attached to a spigot in the yard. A shovel sat in black dirt inside an enclosed garden that sprouted cabbage, tomatoes, and cucumbers. She grabbed the hose—it had a spray head, so that would help. Cranking the water on full, she ran to the garage, as close as she could get, and opened up the spray.

Not a huge garage—maybe sixteen feet deep, twelve feet wide, one door, so big enough for a truck, maybe a workbench. But the propane tank attached to it spilled out gas onto the ground, burning in a puddle and she made sure not to touch it with the water. The fire chewed through the roof, the flames licking out thirty feet into the air. It charred the birch trees surrounding the property, and the heat bubbled the rubber seat of an old snowmobile parked outside.

No saving the garage, of course, so she focused on dampening the sparks and kicking down the fire at the roofline, then moving to the grass around the garage.

More sparks, however, flew in the wind.

"What can I do?"

Crispin, behind her. She pointed to the shovel. "Dig a line around that propane puddle—keep the fire from spreading."

He grabbed the shovel. "Where?"

"About six feet from the edge—make it wide enough so it won't jump. About three feet."

The smoke turned gray, cluttered the yard, and she coughed. Pulling her handkerchief down around her mouth, she turned to the house and started to spray the roof. It hadn't caught fire yet, so if she could wet it, she might save the house, contain the fire to the garage.

Behind her, Crispin grunted, digging fast. She sprayed down the side of the house, then the grass around it. When she glanced at Crispin, he'd already dug a five-foot trench rounding to the back of the tank.

He might have made a good hotshot.

She turned back to the house.

"You're on fire!"

Jerking around, she spotted him barreling toward her.

He grabbed the hose from her and turned the spray on her.

The blast hit her like a fist, cold and fierce, shoving her to the ground. "What are you doing?"

"Your shirt was on fire!"

And now she was drenched too. She rolled, got up, breathing hard. Shucked off her flannel shirt.

"You okay?" He turned her around.

She jerked away. "I'm fine—let's get this fire contained."

He frowned at her, but she stepped away, turned the water onto the house again. "Finish digging that line!"

He said nothing, ran back to his project.

Shoot. Maybe he'd seen her skin. Oh well. The water might protect her from more sparks.

When she finished the house, she turned back to the garage. The roof had caved in, just the frame standing, the fire subsiding. The propane puddle burned hot, but the air dissipated the fumes, and Crispin's line held. She turned her spray to the area outside the line.

Smoke blackened his face, and sweat trickled down into his shirt collar. And still, the man was terribly, devastatingly handsome, dressed in black, a warrior against the flames.

"You okay?" he asked again, now coming over.

"Yeah. Check on Henry." She turned back to the house one more time.

"We need to get moving."

She nodded, but he didn't move. And aw, when she turned, his gaze hung on her back.

"That looks like a bullet wound," he said tightly. Clearly, her white shirt clung to her body. Nice.

"It's fine." She shut off the water.

"It's not fine. You're bleeding."

"Because you sprayed me!" She walked over to the garage now and doused the fire again, and fresh, dark-gray smoke billowed up. "The water opened up the wound."

"You should have let me doctor it at the house."

"I don't need doctoring."

"Now who's the tough guy?" He walked over to his trench and started to throw dirt on the propane flames, killing the fire. The garage fire sizzled, the beams charred, the smoke dissipating in the soggy air.

She turned off the water. "Listen. We have more important things to do than worry about a little scrape—"

"Says the woman who bribed me with food to take a nap on the sofa."

"You needed the nap."

"And you need stitches."

"I don't. It's not as bad as it looks."

He gave her a hard look. "I knew I shouldn't have let you come with me."

Her mouth opened. "Seriously?"

He sank his shovel into the ground. "I don't want you getting hurt—"

"For the love." Then she shut off the hose, looked at him, and took off her shirt.

His mouth opened.

"Please. This is my running bra. But—" She took a breath and turned. "See? Barely a scratch."

She'd seen it in the bathroom mirror, so she knew exactly what he saw—a scrape along her shoulder, the width of a pinky finger, maybe a half inch deep. So yes, stitch-worthy, but she'd had worse.

Which probably, he also saw, because he went very, very quiet.

Yep, those were third-degree burns down her back, healed, the skin still rumpled and shiny.

She pulled her shirt back on, struggling a little since it was still sopping wet. Then she rounded on him.

He swallowed.

"I was in a fire when I was eight years old. Burned twenty percent of my body, so my back, my shoulder. But that was then, this is now, so let's keep moving."

She ignored whatever look or comment he might deliver and headed to the back, re-coiled the hose, and then went into the house.

Henry lay on the sofa, ice pack on his wound, eyes closed, and for a second—"Henry?"

Not dead. He opened his eyes, looked at her. Frowned. "You look so familiar."

"Jade Ransom."

"Jade. Right. You have a brother. Jed." He made to sit up, winced. "I remember you. Firefighter at Wildlands Academy."

She crouched next to him. "Let me see that wound." The wound had clotted, leaving just a terrible welt turning purple on his head. "How'd you get this?"

"A bar across the forehead as I came into my cabin. It could have been worse—I got my hand up. And I got a shot off. But I couldn't stop them from getting away."

"Do you have superglue?"

"Yes," Henry said. "Kitchen junk drawer."

"Let's close up that wound—"

"And then we need to go after them." Crispin had come in behind her.

She got up, and he put a hand on her arm as she walked by. "You too."

Her mouth pursed. But she found the glue in the midst of a drawer filled with screws and tape and wire and a hammer and some lighters.

Henry was sitting up, Crispin beside him.

"You hold the wound shut, I'll glue it," said Jade.

"Sorry, Henry," Crispin said as he pinched the edges together. She applied the glue.

"I'm just glad to see you, Ethan. I was hoping you'd come."

"It would have helped if you'd told me where you were hiding."

Jade had found a bandanna hanging on a hook near the door and now handed it to Crispin. He folded it and put it around Henry's wound.

"I wasn't sure you were still alive, so I didn't want to send my location until I knew you were in town. And then…" He got up. "I was in the hospital." His jaw tightened. "Surgery."

He lifted his shirt and revealed a healing scar across his chest. "Lung cancer. I'm living on borrowed time, kid. Time to end this thing."

Then he walked over to a bench by the door and pulled out a gun.

No, a lethal-looking Springfield AR-10 semiautomatic rifle.

Just like that, he morphed from the sweet old man she'd known, with a floppy-eared hound dog, to an older version of Crispin, probably, still fierce and capable. Gandalf, facing the Balrog. "Let's go."

"Not until I look at Jade's wound," said Crispin. He held the glue, raised an eyebrow.

"After we save the world, okay, Tough Guy?" Then she pushed past Henry, into the yard.

Henry came out, Crispin behind him, shaking his head.

And maybe it was her pride. Or just stubbornness. But the last thing she wanted was him taking another good look at her back, maybe starting to ask questions.

"What is your problem?" Crispin came off the porch. "And I know this isn't life-threatening, but seriously—"

"Fine!" She rounded on him. "I don't need your pity, okay. I don't need you looking at my wounds and thinking…oh, poor Jade. And then suddenly you don't see me as…well, as—"

"The capable, smart, brave woman that you've proved yourself to be?" His mouth tightened. "Has it occurred to you that maybe your wounds are only *proof* of that?"

Oh.

She drew in a breath.

Behind her, an engine had fired up. She looked over to see Henry at the helm of a four-seat utility vehicle. "Get on. You two can have a lovers' squabble on the way."

Lovers' squabble?

Even Crispin raised an eyebrow. But he climbed into the backseat of the vehicle.

She took the front.

And ignored Henry's smile as they motored down a trail in the woods.

This was all sorts of out of control.

Crispin gripped the sidebar of the ATV, holding on as Henry put the gas down, flooring it over ruts and breaking branches and plowing a hole through a worn trail in the woods.

Overhead, smoke mottled the sky, turned the woods hazy and difficult to navigate. Ash and smoke littered the air the farther east they drove. So, clearly, into firestorm country.

"How far is it?"

"About a mile," Henry shouted over the roar. "There's a cave system—I have a place there."

"You hid the missile in a cave?"

"No. A silo—it was already built into the ground. An old minuteman missile silo. Montana is lousy with them."

They emerged from the forest, the terrain turning rocky, mountains rising from either side. They drove through a gorge of sorts, perhaps a dried riverbed, although the boulders seemed struck from the side of the mountain, the size of the Kia he'd stolen.

He'd have to track down the owner, send an anonymous money order.

In the front seat, Jade also braced herself, one hand on the bar, the other on the dash—they probably needed seatbelts.

Then again, she was tough.

Her accusation still simmered inside him. *I don't*

*need your pity, okay. I don't need you looking at my wounds
and thinking...oh, poor Jade.*

As if. But maybe...sure, if he let her story find
root, his heart might turn a little at an eight-year-old
going through the torture of burn treatments and skin
grafts. But now, of course, her words about *surviving
today* made sense.

So maybe she was a little fireproof, like the burnt
area of a forest fire, already having suffered the
flames. And no wonder she faced life the way she did,
the wounds of a bullet shot—or a gunfight, or a house
fire—glancing off her.

Or at least, they seemed to. And yes, it made him
respect her just a little more. But he'd shoved the glue
into his pocket because they weren't done yet.

Henry drove them to a flattened place inside the
gorge, a rocky area where bloomed purple
wildflowers and tall grasses. He slowed, then pointed
to a rusted metal door in the ground.

A trail led to the door, up from a dirt road in the
distance, although hard to make out in the hazy air.
"Had to back the trailer in here, but it's tucked back
in here good," he said. "Hard to spot. Maybe they
haven't found it."

He stopped the ATV, and Crispin barreled out,
running to the metal door. Six feet wide, it had square
handles protruding from two sides. "It looks cleaned
off."

Henry came over, Jade just behind him, as if she
might catch the old man if he went down. But Henry
was part cowhide, part old-school tough. For a
second, an ancient fondness rose inside Crispin.

The man had saved his life. Protected him, in his
way, from the rogue CIA faction.

Henry bent down and grabbed a handle, Crispin the other. They lifted together.

The door opened with a grinding shriek. Inside, rusty corrugated-metal stairs led down into a cement bunker.

"Where's the missile?" Crispin had pulled out the Glock he'd picked up from Henry's place. He'd left the Browning in the four-wheeler.

Henry glanced at him, nodded. "This is the bunker that leads to the missile silo." Then he headed down the stairs. Jade followed. Darkness swathed the corridor as he closed the door behind him, but Henry had flicked on a light.

"The bunker is connected to a grid—and a generator—by underground electrical lines," he said. He walked up to a door, put his hand on it. "This is the blast lock area, one of four 6,000-pound blast doors. It withstands over 1,000 psi of pressure. FYI, a tornado blows a house down with about 5 psi." He was opening the door with a boat-like round handle. The door opened, clearly weighted well on its hinges, and they entered another room, this one small, with a punch-pad code on the next door. "This is the entrapment area of the blast block. You can't open both doors at the same time." He closed the door they'd walked through, then pushed a code, and the next blast door opened.

"Where's the missile silo?"

"On the other side of the door. The door to the old silo was six tons and had a mechanical opening operated by the launch center. Which of course, if opened, activated a security alert at NORAD. My pickup would only haul two tons, so I had the door changed out and the security alert disabled." He shook his head. "Probably a bad idea."

He opened the second door. A long, round tunnel extended maybe fifty feet underground.

"The missile is at the end of this tunnel," Henry said.

Crispin ducked his head in and headed down the tunnel, his gut a fist. Because even from here he could make out the empty silo chamber.

But his breath still caught as he came to the end.

"Is the pad empty?" Henry said.

Crispin stepped inside, looked up. Sixty feet down, the chamber measured maybe ten feet wide. And at the top, the door hung open, smoke clouding the view.

"Yes," Crispin called back. He wanted to hit something. If only —

Jade had followed him down the tunnel. She came out and stood beside him, her voice small. "What does this mean?"

"It means The Brothers have the missile and are enroute to selling it to the Russians," Crispin said, his jaw tight. "It means we have to find it and stop them."

She inhaled. "Okay. But how?"

"There's a tracking device on the missile," Henry shouted — so, clearly their voices had carried. "We can activate it in the launch room."

They scooted back down the tunnel, and Crispin closed the door behind him while Henry opened the next one. A cement hallway led toward the stairwell where they'd entered, then down another tunnel and into the launch room. They came out to a space with bunks built against the rounded walls, a table, chairs, and a small kitchen. A rounded stairwell extended from the middle. They took the stairs up to the second story.

A launch room with screens and computers, and it looked like something out of the eighties, with fat monitors and wide consoles.

"None of this is hooked to anything. Except this." He walked over to a laptop and powered it up.

A flatscreen hanging on the wall also lit up, and in a moment, GPS flickered, illuminating a red dot on the screen.

"It's not moving," said Jade. "I wonder why."

"That's one of The Brothers' encampments," Crispin said grimly.

Henry sank down into a nearby straight chair.

"You don't look so good," Jade said, crouching in front of him.

Crispin didn't feel so good either. "We need to go."

"He needs a hospital. Probably a CT," Jade said.

"I'm okay," said Henry. "Let me pull up a map." He scooted his chair to the laptop and began to type.

Jade got up.

Crispin stalked away, just trying to breathe. Mission fail. After three years —

"Hey." She came up behind him, softly, her hand to his back. "You don't look so good either."

He closed his eyes. "This isn't happening. I can't have died for three years only to have this..." He turned to face her. "If we fail —"

"We won't fail," she said and put her hands on his arms. "God hasn't brought you this far to let you fail."

He gave her a wry look. "That's hope more than theology, right?"

"Hope is how we survive. How we say 'It is well with my soul.'"

He wanted to believe it. Wanted to sink into her gaze, to pull out of her that faith that seemed so tangible, so...real.

And maybe that's why he let his emotions unleash, why he found himself stepping up to her, his gaze searching her face.

Why he cupped her face.

She gasped, something small, and her mouth parted.

That was enough of a yes for him to bend down and kiss her. Maybe a little desperate, maybe a little unhinged, but he kissed her hard, needing that hope from her, and maybe even the crazy calm that she always seemed to exude, but...

Yes, in this moment, right now, everything washed away, and it was simply her, kissing him back, centering him, stilling his racing heart.

And maybe restarting it also, to a different rush, a different hammer of adrenaline.

She tasted of the coffee she'd had for breakfast and smelled of woods and fire, and when she put her hands on his chest, then fisted his shirt, he just wanted to put his arms around her, pull her tighter, maybe pick her up and set her on one of those abandoned desks and dive in.

Except—no. *No*...aw, what was he *doing*?

Because even as he pulled away, even as she looked up at him with those beautiful golden-brown eyes...

He was just going to hurt her. And maybe it wouldn't be because terrorists killed her on his watch, but he had a life, a *solo* life and...

"I'm sorry," he said softly and stepped away. She frowned.

Then Henry put a fine point on it when he said, "So, are we going to stay down here and snog, or save the world from terrorists?"

Right.

Oh, he was a jerk.

Suddenly, she smiled, stepped away from Crispin, grabbed his hand and said, "Door number two, Henry. Let's go."

And bad, *bad* Crispin, because he gripped her hand all the way down the tunnel, into the corridor, until they reached the stairwell and emerged into the sunlight.

And even then, as they hopped in the ATV, he wanted to reach for her and simply hold on.

EIGHT

Even Jade could see they'd dived in headfirst and gotten in way over their heads. "Now what?" She directed her question to Crispin, who crouched next to her behind a cluster of birch trees.

They'd driven back to Henry's smoking homestead, then piled into Crispin's truck and taken it southwest some ten miles, toward an old wildlife refuge where the GPS had ticked The Brothers' location.

After parking deep in the woods, they'd hiked a quarter mile or less and found a surveillance spot just outside the perimeter of the yard.

Henry had made himself small behind a boulder some twenty feet away, but really, with the thick of trees and bramble that surrounded The Brothers' encampment, and the amount of attention paid to their newest member — Fanny, the Phoenix nuke — no one seemed to be worried about witnesses.

Then again, the AK-47s the handful of brothers wore slung over their shoulders seemed a sufficient deterrent.

Especially since between them they had a

shotgun, a Springfield AR-10 semiautomatic, and a Glock. So, yeah, super evenly matched. From a fire watchtower, two armed men wearing military fatigues stood guard, watching over the truck parked in the yard and, more specifically, the trailer attached to it that held Fanny.

She wasn't as big as Jade had thought—the size of a short telephone pole, no markings that screamed *I'm a nuclear missile that could destroy the world.* Or at least the northwest corner of Montana. Fanny sat strapped on a flatbed trailer, hitched to an older model Ram truck. Men were securing a tarp over the missile. Because, you know, traveling down the road with a rocket might attract attention.

"Now we stop them," said Crispin, his tone dark.

It only raked up the moment in the silo when he'd apologized—*apologized*—for kissing her.

What-*ever.*

Except, maybe *she* should be the one apologizing. She could have stepped away, could have been less enthusiastic.

But he'd tasted so good, and frankly, he'd seeded that moment with his words about how her scars made her capable, smart, and brave. She'd nearly kissed him on the spot.

So no, she hadn't had a hope of pushing him away.

But maybe...yes, bad idea if she hoped to walk away from him unscathed.

"Of course. Except, um, *how*, Batman?"

His mouth twitched. "Still working on that."

"Here's an idea. What if we called your pals at the CIA?"

"No time. We can't let them get away. And we're

on American soil, so we'd have to call Homeland Security."

"Right. So, what—we storm the castle? I'll make a lot of noise, you climb into the truck and drive away?"

He looked at her, a spark in his eyes, as if—

Uh-oh. "I was kidding."

"It could work. Except for the part where you get shot, but...maybe Henry drives the truck and I do the distracting—"

"Because it doesn't matter if *you* get shot."

"Some things are worth—"

"I get it." She held up her hand. "I really do. But maybe we try something that doesn't hinge on you dying." And here it went. "I sort of like having you around."

His gaze landed on her again, and he swallowed. "Jade, I—"

"Don't, Crispin. I like you, yes, and that kiss was fairly epic, despite the brevity, but I know the score. You're a solo act. And I'm headed back to Alaska at the end of the summer."

Something shifted in his eyes—relief? Disappointment? She couldn't place it. Still, "So, no apologizing, but also no panicking, okay, pardner?"

His mouth tightened, but he nodded.

A shot fired, then another, and he jerked as she rounded.

Oh *no*. Henry had risen from his perch and shot one of the men in the yard.

The others whirled, searching for him.

"There's your diversion!"

Clearly Batman read her mind, because he leaped up, running for the truck.

She crouched, not sure who to follow—and decided Henry might be the better choice.

Henry kept firing, the men in the yard taking up defensive positions, and there he went, Batman, leaping into the cab of the truck.

The engine turned over.

That's when one of the bullets hit Henry. He jerked back, slammed onto the ground, and sucked air as the wound bloodied his chest.

In the yard, shouts lifted, and she didn't want to look. Instead, she scrambled to Henry. His blood soaked the loamy soil.

"Protect Fanny," Henry rasped.

Aw, stupid superheroes. But she picked up the gun, and of course, she'd fired a weapon before, but she had no intention of killing anyone, thank you. Instead, she pointed it up, still in the direction of the chaos, and pulled the trigger.

The semiautomatic's burst blew her back, the stock slamming against her shoulder, and she let go of the trigger, the gun falling away.

"Keep shooting," Henry said, groaning.

She scrambled to her knees, picked up the gun, her arm on fire.

And that's when she spotted Crispin, out of the truck, on the ground, going round with a man.

She sucked a breath, set the gun tight against her shoulder, and pulled the trigger again.

The bullets seemed to scatter the men behind defensive positions, and Crispin got the drop on his attacker.

Only then did she see one of the other men level his AK-47 toward her.

She hit the dirt and covered up as he shredded the trees around her.

Who'd thought this was a good idea? She might have screamed—but more shooting and then, suddenly, the barrage died.

She lifted her head to see Crispin running toward her, holding his gun. The other man lay on the ground, so she did the math.

Then Crispin was there, scooting to his knees beside Henry. She had nothing to staunch the bleeding but her own hands, but Crispin ripped off his shirt and wadded it into the wound.

A body shot, and it seemed close to the man's heart. Even now, he wheezed, and she guessed fluid filled his lungs. "We need to get him out of here."

Crispin's breaths came hard to shouts behind them. "Can you shoot?"

"Not really, but I can try—"

Crispin was already hauling Henry up, over his shoulder, fireman style. "Shoot—then run!"

She pulled the trigger, let the gun back her up and puncture the sky, and then turned and fled into the woods behind Crispin. He could move, despite the weight of Henry, but she caught up, turned and fired off more shots as if she might be in a Rambo flick.

Crispin had already dumped Henry in the bed of the truck when she burst out of the woods. Blood covered his torso, his shirt sopping and dripping as he wrung it out.

She hopped onto the back. "You drive." Then, because she'd done it before, she pulled off her own shirt and shoved it into Henry's wound. By some miracle, or maybe just sheer grizzly-bear toughness, the man still breathed.

Throwing a leg over him to anchor him, she pressed her shirt into his wound and grabbed the side of the truck with her other hand as Crispin backed out. She hunkered down, protecting Henry from the debris of branches, and prayed they didn't hit a tree.

Survive today.

For a second, she was waking up in the hospital, on her stomach, her back on fire, her mother's face below her, finding her eyes. *You can survive this. Just breathe. In. Out. God is with you. Breathe.*

"Breathe, Henry."

Crispin shot out into the empty road, then floored it.

Ten miles to Snowhaven.

Crispin made it in six minutes. He slowed a little through town and braked under the timber awning of the hospital, his horn blaring.

Staff came out through the sliding door and crowded the truck.

"We have a gunshot victim!" Jade shouted, and Crispin hopped onto the bed, picking up Henry's shoulders.

The man's eyes had closed, his breaths so shallow they barely registered, but he had a pulse.

He had a pulse. She helped carry his feet off, and a gurney appeared. Emergency staff ran him into the hospital.

For a second, Crispin simply stood, breathing, stripped.

Jade stood beside him, empty, not sure what to say.

Then Crispin whirled around, stalked out past the ER entrance, into the parking lot.

Where—

She scrambled after him.

He kept walking, all the way through the lot to the far woods, as if on a mission.

She didn't catch up, just stayed behind him, her heart banging.

He stopped just inside the edge of the forest, then crouched down and put his hands over his head.

His feral roar stopped her cold. A sound that seemed torn from his soul, primal and angry and lethal.

Then he sat back and braced his elbows on his knees and bowed his head. His breaths staggered out, his shoulders trembled.

Wait. Was he—

She swallowed. Walked over. Sat next to him, facing him.

Yep. Tears on Batman's face. He looked away, his eyes red. His jaw pulled.

Silence. She said nothing. Didn't touch him. Just breathed.

Finally, he sighed. Nodded. Looked at her. "After my parents died, it was on me. The system wanted to put my sister into foster care, but I wouldn't let them. But honestly, I was overwhelmed. My parents were good people, people of faith, and I tried to hold on to that, but…" He shook his head. "Anyway, when I was getting offers from the government, Henry came out to talk to me. Recruit me, I guess, but it didn't feel that way. He asked me questions. Took me out for a burger. Listened to my life and my dreams and…" His eyes closed. "I just needed that, I guess. I really missed my dad."

Oh, she wanted to touch him. Instead, she drew up her knees, folded her hands. Only then did she realize the blood drying on them, turning her skin red.

"Of course I joined the company, and Henry became my boss. He expected great things, and I gave him great things and...and when he saved my life and vanished, I felt like I'd lost my dad all over again."

Her throat tightened.

"It feels like God takes away everything good I love."

His words, soft, broken, swept away her breath.

"Maybe He wants me to suffer."

"Oh, Crispin." She couldn't stop herself now. Her hand went to his arm. "No. But yes too."

His eyes widened.

"God doesn't see suffering like we do—I mean, He knows the hurt and the pain of all of it, from grief to betrayal to physical pain. But suffering can only be endured if we look at it from His perspective. From His character. He is good. All the way through. Whenever I was getting my burn washes or the massages of new tissue or even stretching—all of it was excruciating—my mom would sing to me. Hymns. 'It Is Well with My Soul.' And she'd quote Bible verses. She'd say, this trouble feels big, but it's small and temporary. It is intended for your healing and your good. Sort of her paraphrase of 2 Corinthians 4:17."

"This, and my parents' death, and even the past three years doesn't feel good. It doesn't feel temporary."

"And yet, you survived it. And it's made you smart and brave and capable. And exactly the Batman we need to stop the bad people from doing bad things."

He looked at her. "Batman?"

"Yeah. A superhero who lost his parents only to turn into a protector of the city." She raised an eyebrow. "Has it occurred to you that maybe your wounds were *exactly* what God used to make you into the person you are today?"

He drew in a breath.

"And like I said, God is not a joker. He isn't going to bring you this far only to abandon you now."

"Still trying to figure out if He's been with me at all."

She touched her bloody hand to his and entwined her fingers through his. "What do you think?"

What do you think?

What he thought was that his impulsiveness had nearly gotten her killed.

And that now, their actions had lit a fire under Floyd to dispose of the nuke into Russian hands.

Crispin also thought that, despite the blood and dirt and grime on her body, Jade had a beauty about her that seemed to emanate from her soul. He hadn't even thought about her scars since seeing her back — yeah, bold move back there in the yard of Henry's house, and it had nearly left his brain. Her words, however, had brought the image back.

Gnarled, pink, rumpled skin that extended over her shoulder, down her back, and he'd simply gulped back questions, tried to hide his horror.

He got it, then, why she'd shied away from showing him her wounds. Because if someone didn't know her, they'd see only the suffering.

But just like that, the horror had vanished. Because she wore none of it in her attitude, her life.

Not a victim, a victor. Her suffering had made her stronger.

Now he looked at her. "I think I want to start over."

She raised an eyebrow.

"I don't want to be Crispin Lamb anymore. I'd like to be…well, maybe someone who doesn't have three years of the things in my head clogging up the hope that you're right. That God is with me."

"There's a path for that, Crisp. It's called salvation. It's about exchanging your dead soul for life. And the path is repentance, forgiveness, and belief."

He looked at his hand, bloodied, holding on to hers. Sighed. "Yeah. Well, I can't do that and end this the way I need to."

"No, Crispin. That's exactly what you need to do if you hope to end this."

He gave her a wry eye. His hand released hers. "We need to get cleaned up, find Henry, and then, yes, call in for reinforcements."

She sighed. "Okay. You might want to start with Booth."

Booth. Right. "I told him that I didn't need him."

She had risen. "Of course you did." She held out a hand to him. "But even Iron Man couldn't defeat Thanos alone."

He got up. "Your superhero metaphors are all over the place."

"What can I say? I'm a superhero junkie. Why do you think I'm hanging out with you?" She winked then and headed out into the parking lot.

Why *was* she hanging out with him?

More, why had he let her? But even as he followed her into the ER, he knew—he didn't want her to leave.

Pardner.

Oh boy. But he could still taste the out-of-bounds kiss, and good thing they hadn't been alone. Because being with her, then kissing her, had fed the terrible longing inside until it ranged about his heart.

Yes, he wanted a different life. A new life. And maybe not quite what she suggested—that felt too big a surrender, but...

But he could see himself sticking around Montana. After all, Sophie was here.

Except—*I'm headed back to Alaska at the end of the summer.*

The end of the summer was a long time away. Nearly three weeks.

He could be dead by the end of the day.

So maybe he wouldn't think that far ahead. Just now, to catching up to her. To walking with her into the ER, like they might be a team.

She walked up to the desk and asked about Henry Snow. He'd gone to surgery. Then she'd asked about a gift shop and showers. The receptionist had hesitated until, "We're with the Jude County firefighting team. As you know, our HQ was torched. Along with our locker room."

The receptionist made a call, and a nurse showed up to escort them to a locker room with private showers.

"I'll grab us a couple T-shirts," he said as she stepped into one of the shower closets with a towel. She'd already taken off her shoes.

"And pants, if they have them."

He headed down the hall, picking up his cell phone on the way and dialing Booth.

"Is this you?" Booth's voice sounded tired.

"You get a lot of unknown calls?"

"Where are you? Have you found Henry?"

"Yeah. And the…package. But Henry's been shot." He kept his voice low, nodded to a couple nurses. The hospital had adopted the rock-and-timber aesthetic of Montana, with teal blue mountains against a sunburst sky painted on the walls. Groupings of leather furniture in front of massive picture windows looked out to the Kootenai forest to the north, the wide river running through the town just beyond the parking lot, past the woods.

Clearly the small town had obtained outside funding.

He followed the smell of coffee to the gift-shop area.

His stomach suddenly woke up and growled. Inside the gift shop, he found T-shirts and sweatshirts and leggings. He guessed her size and bought a shirt and sweatpants for himself too.

He also grabbed a couple coffees and a bag of beef jerky, then returned to the shower rooms and set her clothes outside the door.

The shower still ran, and from the inside lifted singing.

Wow, he loved—liked, *liked!* her. But maybe he could love her. No, with very little nudging he could love her. Forever and ever and until death did they part.

Which might be anytime, given Floyd and his gang, so…

He stepped into the shower closet, stripped, and

found himself nearly groaning under the hot spray of water. Blood ran off him, pooling at his feet, running into the drain.

He was nearly reborn when he emerged fifteen minutes later in dry, clean clothes, barefoot, and running a towel over his head.

Jade stood in front of the mirror in the main locker area, toweling off her blonde hair too. Tousled, golden, with a slight curl. Her brown eyes met his in the mirror. "We match." She pointed to her shirt—the Snowhaven emblem on the front. "Batman and Robin."

He smiled. "Don't get excited there, caped crusader. This is where I leave my sidekick at the hospital while I fight the bad guys."

She made a face, then threw her towel into a bin. "I get it. I'm not a great shot."

"You're a fantastic shot—if you want to take out trees and scare away rabbits. I think I'll need something a little more accurate for the next part." He threw his towel into the bin.

Then he turned to her. She stood barefoot too and looked up at him.

A beat.

And then, aw, because he didn't know how this might end, and who knew if he'd see her again—and maybe that was simply selfish, but he couldn't help it —he reached for her.

She practically leaped into his arms, embracing his neck, her feet on his, rising up to meet his kiss. No, to practically inhale him, her touch urgent. She almost instantly deepened her kiss.

Catch up, buddy. He pulled her close, then yes,

because she was so much shorter than him, lifted her onto the counter in front of the big mirror.

Stepped closer, her face at less of an angle, one arm around her waist, the other braced against the mirror as he dove in.

A sound, something of desire but sweet, almost pleasure, emitted from her, and oh, it did nothing to help him slow down, to calm his racing heart.

Jade.

She was light and hope and so much more than survival, and right now, exactly what he needed. That touchstone to tomorrow, to the life he'd longed for but had walked away from. And there he was, thinking too far ahead again, but—

She was *life*. Or maybe she simply exuded the spirit of life in her, but just being with her grounded him, and he couldn't let go.

Her arms loosened, just a bit, and she leaned back, away. Met his eyes. "You kiss like you live."

"How's that?"

"Like a man on fire."

"Oh yes," he said, a sort of growl. "It doesn't help that you're so breathtakingly beautiful." He put his other arm around her, ran it behind her back, bent to kiss her again, but she drew in a breath. He froze. "Did I hurt you?"

She exhaled on a smile. "No. Just, I'm not used to…I…well, the truth is, I haven't kissed anyone for a long, long time. And never like this."

He couldn't stop himself. "Good."

She raised an eyebrow.

Oh boy. He closed his eyes, winced, then opened them. "Do you think…after all this is over…"

She met his eyes, started to nod—

His phone buzzed in his pocket. He bit back a word and pulled it out.

"Ethan Tucker?"

He stilled. "Who's asking?"

"My name is Logan Thorne, and I work for President White. We just got a ping that his uncle Henry was entered into the system—a hospital in Montana. And you're the contact on his file."

President Isaac White? Suddenly it all made sense—he'd heard about the assassination attempt on White. No wonder Henry had gone into hiding. Maybe the entire White family was at risk.

"I am Ethan," Crispin said, not sure how to explain anything else.

"Okay then, we need a status report on Henry, and we're sending a man your way. Can I count on you to stay with him until we get there?"

Aw. "Make it snappy," he said. "There's a nuke on the loose."

Silence. Then, "We'll be there by the end of the day." He hung up.

"Who was that?" Jade asked, sliding down from the counter.

He stared at his phone, then looked at her. "I think that was reinforcements."

"Go Justice League," she said and held up her fist. "I knew God would come through."

He met her fist. But, huh.

Maybe.

NINE

Do you think...after all this is over...

Crispin's question simply ran through Jade's brain, over and over and—

Along with, well, *breathtakingly* beautiful?

Oh boy.

It didn't help that all she could think about was kissing him. The hunger of his touch, the way he made her feel at once beautiful, wanted, and yet safe, as if he...

As if he respected her as much as he needed her.

Yes. Maybe after this was over—

"He's awake, but you'll have to wait until he's been transferred to a patient room to see him." The words from one of the med-surg nurses made Jade turn from where she stood at the window overlooking the smoke building in the distant forest. It seemed darker, closer, and maybe she should call HQ, make sure that the team hadn't been called out.

Meanwhile, behind her, Crispin had spent the last hour pacing a trail across the carpeted flooring.

"Thank you," Crispin said now to the nurse.

"You're like a tiger in a cage," Jade said. "Sit down."

He folded his hands behind his neck, sat on a straight-back chair, and let out a groan. "By now, the Russians could have gotten their hands on Fanny, could be headed for a major metropolitan area."

She sat next to him, put her hand on his knee. "It'll be okay."

"Said the pilots as terrorists took over their planes."

"Oh my, we're there."

"We've been there for three years."

"So, let's just take a breath."

He looked at her. "I don't know how you can be so calm."

She lifted a shoulder. "I told you—because once you've been burned, you've already been through the worst."

He offered a wry smile. "I thought you were being metaphorical."

"I know. But it's true—both in reality and in theory. And at the end of the day, I believe God's grace is enough to carry us through."

"My mom used to say that. Nothing is so heavy that God can't take our burden from us."

"There's a verse about that."

"I'm sure there is." He sighed. "Is there a verse about wishing you could roll back time and start over?"

"No. But there's one about how we have no idea what good God has in store for us. No eye has seen, no ear has heard, no mind can imagine what God has planned for those who love him. My paraphrase, but it's something like that. It's what keeps me moving forward sometimes."

"Hope."

"Always."

He sighed. "Another of your mother's verses?"

"Yes." She liked that he remembered.

"She sounds like a great mom."

"She is. She lives in Boise with my dad. I was the surprise of the family—she never thought she'd have another child after Jed."

"Jed, the big brother. The one who doesn't approve of you smokejumping."

"Yes."

"Why not?"

She took her hand from his knee, drew in a breath. "Because it's dangerous."

"And hard work. So why do it?"

"Because Jed did."

"And you wanted to be like him?"

"I wanted to save lives like he saved mine."

Crispin arched a brow.

Oh well. "I started the fire that burned me. I had made a fort in my bedroom, and I wanted light. So I got one of the many candles my mom had around the house and lit it. Only, it wasn't a small candle but a tall taper candle, and it started the blanket on fire. And then, when that caught, I dropped the candle, and it lit the carpet on fire too. I tried to get away, but the blanket landed on me."

He had gone still.

"Jed heard me screaming and came into the room. He pulled me out of the fire, put it out, and dragged me out of the house. Then he went to the neighbor's house and they called 911. If he hadn't, our house would have burned too."

"So Jed's not a jerk."

"No. He's just a brother. And he saw what I went through, and I get it. I do wish he'd see what I've done with creating the simulations of fire. We're doing good things at the National Fire Institute. Someday, I hope to really help with wildfire suppression. Save lives." She twisted the ring on her finger, playing with it. "Like this ring tracker."

"That's the prototype you got from your friend?"

"Yes."

"How does it work again?"

"App on your phone, it connects to GPS. A fire supervisor could have one for every one of his crew."

"What about a PLB?"

"This is smaller, and it won't fall off. I'm testing it on my crew in Alaska."

"Hence your summer gigs in Alaska."

And here went nothing. "I love Alaska. But...I could also—"

"Mr. Tucker, Henry is asking for you." The nurse walked in, and Jade sat back, her words suddenly thick and wedged in her throat.

"We just moved him to a room down the hall." She gave him the number.

He got up. "This conversation isn't over."

Then he took her hand.

Oh. Well. Okay then.

But what if—what if she stayed in Montana? And what? Lived happily ever after with a man who she'd known for three days?

Please.

Still, Crispin had a pretty firm grip on her hand.

He knocked at the door and then opened it. Henry sat in the bed, looking a thousand years older than when they'd walked out of the bomb silo only hours ago. Okay, even then he'd appeared rough, but now an IV protruded from his arm, and he wore an oxygen mask and had dressings on his chest and a bandage around his head.

"Not too long," said a male nurse as he walked past them. Then stopped. "Crispin?"

Crispin wore a wry smile. "Hi, Nick."

"This one stays put," Nick said. Crispin made a noise as he nodded.

"What was that about?" she asked, but Crispin was pulling up a chair beside Henry's bed.

"I got a call from someone named Logan Thorne, who told me you're the president's uncle."

Her mouth opened. No wonder he'd been pacing.

Henry sighed. Nodded.

"Which is why you hid instead of coming forth with the nuke, right?"

Henry reached up a suddenly frail hand and moved the mask aside. "After our department was nearly decimated, I knew the faction wasn't just taking out the team but that, most likely, I was the target. My nephew had just been inaugurated, and the details of the assassination attempt were just coming out, and I thought...they're still out there. So I took myself—and Fanny—out of play. As far as I know, Isaac shut down the Phoenix program. She's one of a kind."

Crispin nodded.

"You have to know, Ethan, how terrible I felt after I wiped your identity. I stole your future, your past, your family—I did it to save your life, but...I know what you lost."

Crispin drew in a long breath.

"That's why I bought the land for your sister and moved her here. Sure, I wanted to watch over her, but I thought it might be the one thing I could do for you."

He swallowed, looked away. "Yep."

"When this is over, you can walk away. You're still dead. You can stay dead."

Crispin looked at Jade. "Or maybe, start over?"

Everything stilled inside her.

"Sure. Whatever you want, I can make it happen."

He looked back at Henry. "Okay, so who is this Thorne?"

"He runs a private off-the-books group that is tasked with taking down threats against our country. Specifically, right now, the Petrov Bratva. They've been behind numerous attacks on our country. They'd like nothing more than to detonate a nuclear missile inside America and blame it on the Russians. Which, of course, is true, but—"

"Would only provoke a war," Jade said.

Henry tapped his nose, then replaced the oxygen mask.

"Logan says he's sending a man here—probably for security reasons, but we need to grab that nuke before Floyd hands it off to someone named Igor." Crispin got up. "But I can't leave you—"

"I'm fine, kid," Henry said through the mask.

"Yeah, well, I'm tired of people dying—or trying to die—on my watch." He gave Henry a pointed look. Then Jade.

"What? I didn't do anything."

129

"Exactly. When you shoot a gun, aim better."

"I aimed exactly where I wanted to aim."

He held up a hand. "It's fine. I just...wish I had eyeballs on the compound to see if they've moved it."

Eyeballs. "What about a drone?" Jade said.

He stopped pacing. "A drone. You have a drone?"

"The team does. I bet we can get Conner to launch it." She pulled out her cell phone. Finally, a signal.

Conner picked up on the second ring. "Jade?"

"Hey, is there any way we can fire up the drone?" She'd walked to the window, and before he spoke, she knew his next words.

"It's already in the air. We've had a flare-up, and we need to call you in."

Yeah, she saw it—the billowing clouds of blackened smoke clogging the air, the fire nearly visible as it crowned across the tree line. "How far is it from Snowhaven?"

"Twenty some miles. But—"

"Yeah, I know. Late in the day, high winds...could be a week, could be tonight."

"The entire hotshot contingency is out on the line. We just need more people fighting this."

"I'm on my way." She shut the phone. "I gotta go."

"I heard," Crispin said. He looked at Henry, something of pain on his face.

"Go, kid," Henry rasped. "You didn't come this far to fail."

Crispin frowned, then nodded.

"Just try and not get dead, okay? The paperwork is a nightmare."

Even Jade smiled as they walked out the door and ran down the hall.

He didn't know what was worse—the fire engulfing the town, or Russians wandering around the country with a nuke.

The nuke, *definitely* the nuke.

But as Crispin stood in the Ember fire command center and watched the real-time screen of the fire's progression—along with a few helmet cams from the teams on the line—broadcast to flatscreens in the command room, he sort of wanted to bring Jade with *him*.

Instead of watching her kit up to jump into an inferno.

Who was this woman?

She came walking down the hallway to HQ, having changed into her canvas pants and yellow Nomex shirt. "Did you get a glimpse of the compound?"

She'd introduced him to her boss, Conner Young, and the incident commander, Miles Dafoe, an older guy who seemed to have a calm handle on the conflagration.

A topographic map of Kootenai National Forest hung on the wall, with pushpins of various hotshot teams deployed in the field. They'd brought in teams from Idaho, Alaska, Minnesota, and even southern Montana. And if he understood the chatter correctly, they'd also deployed airplanes and choppers from the area to bomb the fire with water and slurry.

He knew what his request had cost them, but Conner had obliged and directed the drone operator to fly it north to the coordinates Crispin had given.

The compound was, of course, empty, and Crispin leaned on the back of a chair and hung his head.

He'd finally walked out into the hallway and leaned against the wall, trying to sort out his next move. Oh, he wanted to put his fist into a wall, but...

Well, but Jade had come walking down the corridor with her question. He managed a dark shake of his head.

She grabbed his hand. "We'll find them."

Just like that. *We'll find them.* Oh, he wanted her faith.

But tragedies like Oklahoma and 9-11 told him differently.

They walked into the room to a weather report from Miles. "Winds from the north have whipped up the wall of flames. We're getting reports of a running crown fire, moving downhill. We're pulling the teams out and digging a road here, along the river to the north of town, and moving incident command over to the Snowhaven fire department. It's got a parking lot big enough for a chopper, and the airport is right across the street."

Jade stepped up to the map. "If we start a back-burn here"—she pointed to a thin service road marked as *Shelly Mountain Trail*, so narrow it had only a penciled name—"we can burn out the fuels to the north, meet it head-on."

"It's burning so fast it'll jump that," said Conner.

"Maybe not, if we can burn out the fuel in front of it. Then we extinguish it at the trail." She looked at Conner. "We have to try. If it keeps growing, it jumps your line in front of the Kootenai River, and then it's a free-for-all into Snowhaven."

Even Crispin could see she was right.

"That's really close to the fire head," Miles said. "You'd have to put down here, at Penny Creek Campground, and hoof it a quarter mile southwest. But it's still far enough from the fire you should be clear. If not, do not proceed."

"Yes, sir."

He blew out a breath, stared at the map. "Okay, if you get into trouble, this is your safety area. Penny Lake. The trailhead to the river is about a half mile south of your drop, and it leads to a river. So if you get there, you can follow the river to the lake. The river is too shallow for real safety, so keep moving." He shook his head, his jaw tight. "You start the burn, keep it under control, but no mistakes, Jade."

"Yes, sir. No one dies today."

"Let's get a look at that landing area, CJ," said Miles, now leaning over the drone guy.

CJ guided the drone over to the coordinates. A cleared field shone on the screen.

"That's more than a campground," said Crispin.

"It's an old farm turned glamping area," said Conner. "Lots of cleared land."

Crispin stepped closer and leaned over the man's shoulder. "That's a truck. Can you get over that truck?"

CJ flew the drone closer and Crispin froze. "That's—" He glanced at Jade. "*Them*." Three men, and one looked up and spotted the drone. Pulled out a handgun.

"Uh-oh," said CJ, and he angled the drone up and away, even as the man shot at it.

"Whoa," said Miles. "What's with that?"

"Stay on it, CJ," said Crispin as he watched the

men climb into the truck. Another truck followed, and they pulled out toward the thin mountain road.

Crispin looked at Jade. "I have to go."

"Me too." She grabbed a walkie.

"Stay safe, Jade," Conner said.

Crispin followed her out of the room, down the hall. Voices emerged from the ready room, her team getting ready.

He grabbed her arm. And then, because...well, because this could all go south, for either of them, he pulled her into a darkened office. Shut the door.

Dim light shone through a side window.

He stared at her. She looked up at him.

"I want to tell you not to go," he said.

"Right back at you."

He swallowed. "I can't...I don't..." He closed his mouth, looked away, hated how his chest tightened.

Of course, she saved him again. "I know..." She touched his chest. "I know it's only been three days, but I guess I'd like at least three more."

He looked at her. "And three more after that?"

She nodded. "Who knows what—"

"Yeah. Exactly. Who knows what tomorrow might bring?"

She kissed him. Just like that, and yes, he was right there, all in. He wrapped his hand around her neck, brought her to himself, and kissed her back. Fiercely. Possessively. And full of the terrible, brilliant, terrifying hope that everything she believed —everything he wanted to believe—might be true.

That God had more for him. That a good, new day awaited. And that providence just might—please—be on his side.

He let her go, breathing hard.

She nodded. "No one dies today."

He shoved out the door and didn't look back.

He probably needed Booth, but his partner was fighting a fire, and maybe, if he did this right...

Aw, there was barely a hope that this would go well. But still...

A hope.

The smoke clogged the sky as he got into his Ford and tore out of the lot. On the tarmac, a female pilot walked around her small plane. A few of the smokejumpers had jogged out, carrying helmets and packs, axes and chain saws and shovels.

He turned his truck north and floored it up the highway to Snowhaven.

He'd memorized the map, so he took the road outside the town, toward the bridge over the river, then cut northeast on a dirt road that wound into the woods. Here, the haze of the fire hung low, and the dirt his truck kicked up didn't help visibility. But the truck hauling Fanny would be hard to miss.

He thought a plane droned overhead but couldn't see it, so maybe it was just his pulse in his head. *Please, God*—he didn't know what else to say, really. Okay, maybe, *"Protect her."*

Three more days. And three more and...

He just had to survive today.

The sound of a heavy engine ahead made him hit his brakes, and then, as he came over a rise, he spotted it, down the road a half mile.

Henry's old blue Ram truck, ferrying Fanny to her new owners.

Another truck kicked up dust behind it.

Here went nothing. Crispin unhooked his seatbelt, then punched the gas.

C'mon, swerve.

The truck kept coming, and of course, his little F-150 wasn't a match for the power of the Ram, but it could slow it down and maybe force it off the road and put the trailer in the ditch and—

The truck wasn't veering.

"C'mon!"

The driver seemed to be panicking, the truck rocking, as if he might be trying to decide—

Crispin kept coming, even as he glanced at the ditch. Hard landing. But he might live through it. How he wished for tactical gear, but he was still wearing the silly sweatpants and T-shirt from the hospital. He'd fixed the problem of where to stash his handgun, but a leap out of the truck would definitely hurt.

The truck had lurched to one side, as if trying to juke him out, like they might be playing basketball.

That's right. He matched it, then back—

The driver jerked the wheel hard—too hard, and suddenly the truck skidded, the swerve too severe, and with the weight of the trailer, the truck's back wheels lifted.

The trailer barreled forward, twisting the hitch, and the truck went over, rolling just as the trailer tore free.

Crispin slammed on his brakes, turning the wheel as the F-150 skidded, barely missing the ditch. Then he slammed the truck into drive, away from the rolling Ram—

Too fast. The F-150 careened into the ditch as the Ram truck settled on its side, a cloud of dust clogging the road.

Fanny's trailer lurched into the forest, bumping

across the ditch, taking out bramble and crashing into a tree before falling on its side.

Fanny jerked from her bonds and rolled away.

She lay in the forest, lethal and free.

Crispin grabbed Henry's rifle and rolled out of the cab just as the following truck roared up behind the rolled Ram.

The Ram lay on its side in the middle of the road, undercarriage forward, and Crispin raced up to it.

A man emerged, and behind him, the driver had gotten out of his truck. "Get down!" This from the second driver, who lifted his AK-47.

Crispin dove for cover behind the truck, the bullets landing behind him, scraping off dirt. But he'd gotten a good look at the man. Long dark hair, beard, an American militant in Russian fatigues.

Floyd Blackwell.

And that's when, overhead, the sound of a small plane burned through the sky.

He glanced up.

Big mistake. The man from the cab launched himself out and over the truck and lunged at Crispin.

Crispin found his feet a second before the man grabbed him around the waist. Big guy, clearly some Russian thug with meaty hands and a good forty pounds on Crispin. He slammed a fist into Crispin's ribs, and Crispin held in a grunt as pain exploded through him.

But he got his elbow in the man's face, exploded his nose, and Igor the Russian rolled off him, shouting.

Crispin spotted the rifle and dove for it, grabbed it, rolling.

The shot hit Igor center mass from eight feet away.

Crispin bounced to his feet, blood on his shirt, his face. He spotted Floyd in the woods as he was trying to pick up one end of the nuke.

"It's over!" Crispin shouted. He lifted the gun to Floyd.

"Nyet." The voice emerged behind him, and he turned. The driver, blood saturating his shirt from a head wound, stood, a little wobbly, on the dirt road outside his overturned cab. He aimed a handgun at Crispin. "Gun down," he said, motioning with his Ruger.

"Finally." This from Floyd, and Crispin glanced over to see that he'd abandoned the effort and picked up his AK-47. "Time to end this."

Crispin stood there, listening to Jade's words. *No one dies today.*

Sorry, babe.

TEN

Oh goody, now she got to watch the man she loved get shot—okay, that might be overstated, but she could see herself falling hard and fast and maybe she was already halfway there for Crispin Lamb.

Brave, intense, addicting Crispin Lamb, who called her beautiful. *Breathtakingly* beautiful.

Focus.

She'd leaned out of the open door of the Otter, along with Duncan, watching as below, on the road, Crispin crouched behind an overturned truck. His Ford sat in the ditch, the trailer overturned in the woods, and somewhere, no doubt, lay Fanny.

But her eyes had stayed on the man with the AK-47 peppering the road with bullets.

She leaned back, breathing hard.

Just survive today, Crispin. Because she had a fire to fight and…

Oh God, please help him!

"Is that Crispin down there?" Booth had come over, also leaning out the open door, one hand on his safety line.

"Yeah."

"And Floyd," said Booth. He sat back. "He's going to get killed."

She looked at him. "Nice."

"I'm just saying—we need to help him."

"There's a fire barreling down on Snowhaven—"

"Yeah. And it's too fast. It's going to jump the road long before we get there." He pointed west to the crowning blaze shooting off the trees, running south. The flame lengths had grown, the fire picking up speed, the breadth of it like a tidal wave, cresting lethal orange and red across the canopy of forest.

Racing south.

Too fast to stop it with her brilliant plan. And if they deployed, she'd only cost lives.

Above the fire, the aerial assault planes dropped water and slurry on the flames, trying to slow the front. Steam rose as single-engine air tankers deployed slurry and rose out of the clutter.

A couple Bombardiers followed with water loads.

Now, she raised her radio, then paused and looked at Booth. "I'm going anyway."

"To do *what*?"

"I don't know—help Crispin?"

"Have you lost your mind?" He was shouting now. "The last thing he wants is for you to get in the middle of this—"

"Yeah, well, the last thing I want is for him to die alone!"

This shook her, and maybe Booth too, because he drew in a sharp breath. "Okay, fine—we both go."

"I'm sending the rest of the team back!" She directed her shout to Logan. "Booth and I are deploying!"

Logan's mouth opened, but she turned away and

spoke into the mic of her helmet. "Aria, get us over the drop zone. Booth and I are going out."

She spotted the field ahead. The fire blazed to the west, the smoke coughing up, black and deep gray, but the campground remained clear.

Aria circled, and Duncan deployed the ribbons.

They fluttered down easily, barely a wind.

She unhooked the safety line, turned back to Logan. "Get the team back! We'll be right behind you!"

He shook his head, but she ignored him, glanced at Booth. "Ready?"

He nodded, also unhooking.

Then she went out the door. Brisk air, freedom, the sense of flying. Only, this time it felt so very long to deploy her chute, grab the toggles, and get down, even though it took less than five minutes.

She had her chute in hand, rolling it up as Booth landed near her in the crispy grass.

Overhead, the plane banked and headed back toward Snowhaven.

Unhooking her chute, she shoved it into her pack, then stepped out of her jumpsuit.

"Leave the packs!" She did, however, pick up her Pulaski and helmet.

Behind her, Booth did the same. She noticed the bear gun on his hip in a small secured holster too.

"He's only a quarter mile down the road," she said and took off running, clearly out of her mind.

She'd never done something so impulsive in her life. But…

But, well, she'd never live with herself if she didn't do *something*.

Booth passed her, running hard as the road

curved westward. Ahead and to her west, she spotted flames spiking out of the forest, burning hard—already past the service road. So, good call to send the team home. She coughed, the smoke thickening here, and pulled her bandanna down over her nose.

Now twenty feet ahead, Booth had pulled out his gun at shots barking ahead.

At the top of the hill, Booth pulled up, darted into the woods. She veered off the road, following him, crashing through the brush behind him. She hadn't realized that sparks dripped from the sky, but they broke from the ashy smoke and dropped on the loam around her, sizzling, dying out.

The fire seemed still a half mile away…still—

Nuclear missile in the woods. Probably a fire wouldn't detonate it, but—

She swiped up her radio, slowed a little to talk. "Team Alpha to Command, this is Ransom."

"Command, come back, Ransom. Did you deploy?"

"No. The head is crowning too fast. Booth and I are on the ground—we need a drop of slurry on the Shelly Mountain Trail, a half mile from our drop site. *Right now*."

A moment of static.

"Jade—the fire hasn't reached Shelly Road—"

"It's on the way. Which is why we need the slurry —trust me!"

Ahead of her, Booth hunkered down behind a tree, breathing hard. He held up his hand to stop her.

"Confirmed," Miles said as she skidded to a crouch beside Booth. Her breaths raked in, and he put a finger to his lips and pointed.

Her heart nearly buckled at the sight of Crispin,

weaponless, picking up one end of the heavy nuke along with another man, a third holding a gun on him.

"That thing is six hundred pounds," Booth said. "There's no way—"

Indeed. Crispin dropped his end, bent over, breathing hard.

The man with the gun cuffed him, and he went down on his knees, catching himself on his hands.

She bit back a shout. Booth drew in a breath. "I can't get a shot."

"You'd better get a shot, because they'll kill him," she snapped.

Overhead, an airplane engine droned—thank you, Miles.

Crispin struggled to his feet. Straddled the end of the missile. The big guy at the other end bent and strained with the load.

Booth stood up. "I think I can get the other guy."

She looked up. Above, a single-engine tanker emerged from the smoke.

"Duck!"

Booth pulled the trigger.

Slurry dumped from the heavens, eight hundred gallons of a mix of water, ammonium sulfate, and red food coloring. Like blood, it splattered the forest, the road, and coated her helmet and body.

Booth dove against the tree, protecting himself.

Shouting erupted, and she lifted her head to see Crispin grappling with a man, both of them slippery with retardant.

Booth must have spotted them also, because he took off running, his feet slippery in the slurry.

She followed, fighting for grip as she ran. Ahead,

the man fighting Crispin lost his gun but rolled and kicked Crispin away as he scrambled to his feet.

Crispin dove for the gun. Lifted it.

It dripped with goo.

The man reached the road, dove into his truck, and plowed into the ditch, past the overturned vehicle, and down the road.

Crispin took off, running hard after him.

Like he might catch him?

"Crisp!" Booth shouted, and he turned. Stared, his gaze ferocious on Booth.

On her.

The fury on his face shook her.

Booth checked on the man lying in the woods, bending over, his fingers to his pulse. "Dead."

Crispin had turned, staring down the road as his assailant left in a wake of dust and smoke.

Then he rounded and ran back to them, breathing hard. "What did you do?" He directed the question at Booth, then her.

She opened her mouth. "Saved your life!"

"He got away!" He pointed down the road. Bloody retardant sat in his hair, saturated his shirt, his pants. "That was Floyd, the head of The Brothers, and he just *got. Away.*"

She stared at him, her breaths hard. "We stopped the fire from reaching the nuke—hello. Isn't that—"

"It wasn't going to go off. The fire would have burned the electronics, but it wouldn't have started a nuclear reaction!" He shook his head.

"Crispin, calm down—"

"No. Three years of—"

"He had you under his gun!" Jade stepped forward. "He was going to kill you."

He rounded on her now, his mouth tight, his jaw pulling. "You shouldn't believe everything you see."

He then lifted his soggy, slurry-drenched shirt.

A gun, taped to his stomach.

Oh.

He let the shirt drop.

"I thought he was going to kill you."

"This is why I work alone." He shook his head. "Now Floyd's in the wind." He walked over to the nuke. "I can't just leave this in the woods. And it's too heavy for us to lift."

"Problem is, we need a ride back to town," Booth said. "The fire is headed to Snowhaven."

"Perfect. Just for once, I'd like to have only one problem at a time." He pulled out his phone from his pocket. "It's dead." He headed back to the truck.

Jade stood in the sopping forest, a spear in her heart.

Booth scrambled behind him, but when she didn't move, he turned. "Let's go. We need to beat that fire back to Snowhaven."

Right. She swallowed the tightness in her throat and caught up.

"Give the truck a nudge, Booth," Crispin said and got inside. He fired up the truck, and Booth pushed it from the back. Jade added her efforts, and the F-150 dug its way out of the ditch.

Booth hopped in the back. Held out his hand to her.

She met Crispin's gaze through the rearview mirror. His mouth tightened, and he looked away.

Fine. She took Booth's hand and climbed onto the bed of the truck. As soon as she sat, Crispin pulled out and tore down the road, the fire closing in behind them.

But Jade already felt burnt clear through to her soul.

Even his pants stuck to his legs. Crispin was a giant slushy, caked in goo, a chill burning through him to his bones.

No, he was a giant slushy *jerk*. Because Jade's flinch as his words had emerged kept rounding in his brain.

She might have saved his life. Probably not—one more knock to the ground and he'd have come up armed, would have dispatched Floyd first, then his Russian pal. But it only went down like that in his head.

In real life, he could have had a cracked skull, been left for dead in the woods while a wildfire bore down on him. Crispy, just like she'd called him.

Right behind that came the memory of her helping him to his cabin, doctoring him out of shock, cooking him a steak. The memory of her tracking down Henry's cabin and then The Brothers, of her manhandling the semiautomatic—or maybe letting it manhandle her—as they escaped. Her covered in blood as she fought to save Henry's life.

The kiss in the bathroom, where she'd lit aflame a future he'd never believed in, never seen coming.

Until her.

He slammed his hand on the steering wheel as he slowed, then turned to cross the bridge. Trucks lined the road on the north side of the river, firefighters in yellow jackets and helmets deploying, armed with saws and shovels. Two bulldozers carved a wider path beyond the paved road, shoving down trees and bramble and overturning grass.

A glance in the rearview mirror, past the two sodden smokejumpers in the back, showed a mushroom cloud of advancing fire.

He needed to fix this. Yes, grab the nuke and find Floyd, but...aw, he'd been frustrated and angry and hurt and—he'd taken it all out on her.

Survive today. What he really wanted was to see beyond this moment to tomorrow. But his vision had always been cluttered, smoky, cloudy—

No eye has seen...what God has planned for those who love Him.

Yes. Maybe he needed to stop relying on his own vision. Start trusting God's.

Crispin pulled up to the fire department in Snowhaven. A small, two-garage-stall building attached to a main area. He spotted the Otter on the tarmac across the street. In front of the fire station, a few smokejumpers peeled out of their gear. It clicked then, that only Jade and Booth had jumped.

Probably after seeing him on the road, pinned down.

Which meant she'd chosen to help him, walk right into a gunfight instead of stopping the fire. And that only tightened his gut, because now she was making choices that could cost lives. Because of him.

Because of *him.*

He wasn't a man of deep emotion, but this had him all clogged up as he put the truck into Park and barreled out of the cab.

She was hopping down from the back, Booth behind her.

"Jade!"

His voice stopped her, and she turned. Her helmet had protected her eyes from the slurry, so he saw clearly the hurt, even anger in them. "I gotta go, Crispin."

"Listen—I was angry—"

"No duh. I get that." She held up her hand. "I get that you're a solo act. You kept telling me that, and I should have believed you, so that's on me."

Oh. "No—I—"

"You're right. If I hadn't gotten involved, jumped out of that plane, sent the slurry, maybe you'd have the nuke in your truck right now, Floyd in handcuffs. Batman saving the world."

He didn't have handcuffs, so probably there would be a different end to Floyd, but now he was just caught up in the details. "Or not—"

"Doesn't matter. I have a job to do, and so do you, and this is where I get off the carnival ride. One less problem for you."

"Jade—"

"Go, Tough Guy. Be super. Save the world. It's been…" She swallowed, and for the first time, he saw her waver, take a breath.

He reached out to her, but she stepped away. "Don't die." Then she whirled and strode away, breaking into a run as she headed toward her team.

"That was epic."

Booth stood there, and only now did Crispin notice him.

"I'm a jerk."

"Yep. Always sort of known that, pal. She was trying to save your life. We both were."

He glanced then at Booth, covered in slime. "Thanks."

Booth pursed his lips, nodded. Sighed. "But now there's a nuke in the woods."

"Yeah."

"And Floyd's in the wind."

"Yeah." He turned. "But guys like Floyd will always be in the wind, cooking up something. One problem at a time."

His gaze landed on Jade, talking now with one of her teammates, gesturing to the fire line. "Jade does not like to be a burden. She's a doer."

"Probably one of the few people on earth who can keep up with you." Booth had taken out a handkerchief, started to wipe his face and neck. "This stuff's like glue."

As he watched, she headed inside the station. "She not only kept up, she was *ahead* of me, so many times."

"I don't know her well," Booth said, "but she seems pretty tough. She'll be okay."

"She's not fireproof, Booth. I hurt her, and…" He made a fist, let out a word.

"Okay then," Booth said. "Fix it. But let's get the nuke secured first. Stay put. I'll be right back."

He took off, jogging toward the group of firefighters. Crispin headed to his glove compartment, where he'd stashed the duct tape and sunglasses and a couple cloths. He took one out and wiped his neck, his face. Booth was right—glue.

Footsteps slapped on pavement, and he turned to see Booth returning with a couple smokejumpers. "This is Logan—you met him at The Brothers' encampment. He's a career firefighter, but he can handle a weapon. And this is Vince." Booth left out any designators, but Crispin had seen him handle a gun, so maybe military in his background. "Think we can carry the package?"

"Let's grab some packing straps." Crispin pointed to a couple crates stacked next to the fire station, black webbing in a pile near them. "I think we can carry her."

"Her?" Booth asked as Vince ran over to retrieve the straps.

"Fanny."

He shook his head. "Pile in guys." He headed for the front passenger door. "The brass is still trying to figure out what to do with us, so let's make it quick."

A quick dash up the road into the headwall of a forest fire. Sounded about right. "Hold on tight." Crispin got in, and the two smokejumpers landed in the back.

Then he backed out of the drive. When he turned the truck around and glanced into the rearview, Jade wasn't standing on the pavement, watching him go.

Yes, he'd royally screwed that up.

The smoke thickened as he crossed the bridge again, then peeled back up the Shelly Mountain Road. He knew it better now and hoped the guys had a good grip on the side of the truck, because he chewed up the dirt, the truck nearly planing out.

He slowed before he reached the slurry drop, not wanting to slide into the forest going eighty. As it was, he nearly skidded into the overturned truck. The boys jumped out, and he turned the truck around, backing halfway into the woods.

Sparks littered the air, falling like droplets around

them, the fire loud now, roaring as it lit the horizon. He guessed it may be five hundred yards away. The tops of the trees exploded, casting branches and leaves into the air, debris cycloning around them.

The slurry acted as a fire shield on his body. Huh —hadn't seen that coming.

But hadn't she said that? God going before him in circumstances he saw as suffering. Intended for his good. Yeah, yeah, he got it now.

Vince and Logan laid the straps down on the ground, and together they rolled Fanny onto them. Then they each took a side and lifted. A hundred and fifty pounds each, and even that turned his body to fire, but they muscled her onto his truck bed. Then the guys jumped in, along with Booth in the back, held it down, and Crispin scrambled back into the front seat.

No one mentioned the dead man, covered in slurry and blood, about to be consumed by the fire.

Sparks lit the road in front of him, and he put the truck into Drive. Glanced up.

The fire had crowned right above him, turning the trees to pyres, burning detritus swirling in the firestorm.

Behind him, the guys were swatting fire as it landed on them. Logan and Vince wore their jackets and helmets, but it wouldn't protect them from—

A tree fell along the ditch, fire popping from the branches. He swerved, and the guys ducked—

They were going to be consumed.

Except—the lake. Where was that lake, their safety point?

Even as he thought it, he spotted the sign to the trailhead. "Hold on!" He slammed the brakes, skidded, and took the trailhead. Tearing through branches, he took off his mirrors, but the fire hadn't caught up yet.

He burst out into an overlook, then a riverbed, a trail leading down it, toward—if he remembered correctly—a lake, still out of view.

But he hoped, oh, he hoped.

Gunning it past the overlook, he bumped down across the riverbed, then took it south, his truck tires crushing the rocks, the river having dried with the summer's heat, leaving only smaller gravel and debris on the shoreline.

The fire spiked through the trees, but he'd managed distance between them. Still, the guys struggled, Fanny rolling around in the back, the guys bracing her with their feet.

He slowed, just a little.

Too much. The fire shot skyward, his entire rearview mirror ablaze.

He kicked it down, turned with the riverbed, and there—ahead, the river opened to a lake. A beautiful, gray-blue lake that just might save their hides.

He pulled up along the shore and piled out, and the guys hopped over the edge. "What about the nuke!" Vince shouted.

"It'll be fine!" Booth shouted back. "But we're about to get crispy!"

He plowed into the water and Crispin followed him. Cool and clean, and it found the grime and slush and washed it away, and then he dove headfirst.

The water rushed over him, into his hair, his pores, through his T-shirt, and only after he'd gone in did he realize he still wore his gun duct-taped to his chest. But it was a Glock, so it should be fine.

And maybe he wouldn't need it. Maybe this was the end—he could let someone else find Floyd. Let it go and start over and…

Hope.

He didn't know why he stayed under. Maybe for the chill to calm his racing heart. Or maybe he simply spotted the flames rimming the shoreline and wanted, just for a moment, to stay out of the heat. But as he did, he seemed to hear a voice. Something solid inside him. *Though you were dead in your sins, God made you alive, with Christ.*

Words, spoken at his parents' funeral, somehow lodged deep inside.

Only to unearth today. Now.

Yes, God. He wanted a new life. A life free of the darkness and sin and doubt and anger and—

Please. Forgive me. Save me.

And then, as if the words themselves had power, something seemed to unlatch from his soul, the abruptness jarring, breathtaking.

He burst out of the water, gulping breath.

The front wall had swept past them, the woods still burning, but his truck had survived, parked on the gravel. A little singed, but still functioning.

And in the bed, Fanny. Sleeping.

Booth let out a laugh, something nervous in it. Logan hung his hands behind his neck, as if stunned, water dripping off him.

Vince just seemed to breathe, glancing at Crispin, shaking his head.

And Crispin…yes. Something had changed. His entire body seemed lighter, healed even.

Something big and glorious and freeing swept through him and took hold.

He wanted to name it…hope.

Hope is how we survive. How we say "It is well with my soul."

That's what he wanted—to be well in his soul, come what may.

"There's a bridge across the river down there," said Logan. "And a road south. Probably back to Snowhaven."

"Let's get back to town," Booth said. "Before the fire takes it out."

And this time when he said it, Crispin lifted his eyes to heaven. *Please, God, keep Jade safe.*

ELEVEN

Focus.

She didn't have time to listen to her stupid bleeding heart. Sheesh, Jade should be thankful she'd gotten out ahead of this thing before she really got burned.

Inside the Snowhaven Fire Department locker room, she shucked off her jumpsuit, heavy with the stupid slurry, and dropped it on the floor, along with her pack. She should rinse it off, but with the state of the fire rolling over the hills, she wanted to get to the command center and listen to Miles's plan of attack.

Anything to get her brain off Crispin, and really, her brain should be on the fire. Not on Crispin.

Or the tight expression of pain as he'd gotten out of the truck and tracked her down. Maybe he'd been about to apologize, but...but frankly, the man had done them both a favor. She wasn't great at not jumping in to save the day, and clearly, as much as he'd held her hand and tried to act like she might be his partner, he'd always be, like he said, a solo act.

Kill this fire, then pack her bags and go home.

She walked out of the locker room into the empty

garage of the fire station. Weird that Logan and Vince weren't here. "Hang tight, guys," she said to the rest of her team. "My guess is that we're going out onto the line."

The incident team had practically lifted incident command from Ember to Snowhaven, complete with computers and the drone, still operated by CJ, who was staring at his computer screen. Another dry-erase map hung on the wall, this one probably under the ownership of SFD, but this time, all the pushpins lined up along the road on the opposite side of the river.

Miles was on the phone, yelling at someone about needing more planes, his legs braced, staring out the picture window.

Nova, too, manned a radio, talking with one of the crew chiefs. "No. Block off the 518. No one goes into the Kootenai." She lifted a hand to Jade.

"So, it's going well then," Jade said to Conner, who held his phone, texting. "What can I do?"

"We have everyone out on the line. We need more personnel, but everyone is deployed. I'm trying to get another dozer up here."

Her gaze had gone out the window to the rim of fire shooting above the treetops, the cloud that ballooned over the horizon. Then she walked to the fire map. "It hasn't jumped County Road 518."

"No," said Miles, coming over. "But it did jump the Shelly Mountain Road, all the way to the river. We caught it on drone." He picked up a marker and blackened in the burnt area, ran a line across the current location.

"The road opposite the Kootenai River is wider than the Shelly Mountain Road, and if you look, the entire conflagration is bordered by the 518. If we can pinch it off here, we have a smaller area to fight."

Miles pointed to the narrowest part of the river. "It could cross here. And then we'll lose the town. We're trying to widen the road across the river."

She stared at the map. "We ran a scenario in our labs like this. A running crown fire where the surface and crown are linked. The surface intensity ignites the crowns and keeps feeding them. But if we can dampen the surface fuels, we can slow the crown run. At least in the sim."

She put her hand on the unburnt area. "This needs to burn."

"I think it will."

She turned to him. "No. I mean we need to burn it. We need a controlled burn, starting along the entire line. We can keep it moving forward, burn out the fuels at the surface, and then when the headwall hits—"

"It's going too fast."

"Not if we slow it down at the source." She pointed to the headwall. "We bombard this with slurry and water, get everything we have into the sky. It'll slow it down, maybe weaken it, and then when it hits the black, it'll have nothing to feed it. We kill it before it hits the line, but even if it doesn't die, it'll be weak enough for us to hit it with the hoses."

Miles nodded, listening, probably calculating planes and personnel.

"It's a good idea," said a voice behind her. "I think it will work."

She turned and stilled.

Her brother Jed, tall and handsome and weary

SUSAN MAY WARREN

around the eyes, came in, sooty in his yellow jacket, a hat, his name written on the breast. J. Ransom.

Just like hers.

"Jed."

"Hey, Jade." He took off his helmet, came over to her. And then he pulled her into a hug. "I'm glad you said yes."

She pulled away, frowned at him. "What?"

"When Nova went down, Conner called me and asked me what I thought about bringing you in. I told him he needed the best crew chief I knew—besides me." He winked. "But this plan…" He walked over to the map. "I think it could work." He glanced over his shoulder. "Apparently that masters in fire behavioral sciences isn't just words on a page." He winked. Looked at Miles. "My guys are in the bus, waiting to deploy."

Miles pointed to the 518. "I have the teams from Ember here and the Juneau team next to them. There's a couple Boise teams working the other side of the bridge." He looked at Jade. "Your plan takes out the old Snowhaven Community Church, just so you know."

"The church isn't a building. They'll rebuild. But we can't rebuild an entire city."

He looked over at a woman, standing with her arms folded. Mid-fifties, she wore the strain of the fire on her face.

"Do it," she said.

Miles turned back to Jade. "You take your jumpers and drip cans and follow the dozer that Conner just ordered all the way to the east end of the line. Grab a couple 'shots from the Ember team if you need help."

"Yes, sir," Jade said.

Jed nodded, then walked with her out to the garage. His Missoula team had disembarked to talk with her jumpers.

"You doing okay, sis?"

"You really recommended me for the job?"

"Had to figure out some way to get you back to Montana. We miss you."

She swallowed, the words landing on raw soil, almost bringing tears. "Yeah. How is Kate?"

"Great. She trained our jump team but is mostly home with JR." His voice lowered. "How are you doing after…you know?"

She stared at him. *You know?* And weirdly, her only thought was of Crispin and the terrible shearing of her heart, and…wait—"You're talking about the fire in Alaska? The flashover?"

"Yeah. Scary. I heard you guys had to get into shake and bakes."

"It was under control."

He looked at her. Then shook his head.

"What?"

"Why do you always have to be the toughest one in the room?"

She blinked at him. "What?"

"Just…" He glanced at his team, then cut his voice low. "I know you can handle yourself out there, I really do. But you don't have to prove anything, okay?"

She had nothing.

"I'm proud of you, sis. Please don't do anything stupid. I'll see you after."

Then he pulled her into another hug.

Huh.

He let her go and rounded up his team. They hopped into a school bus, the words *Missoula Firefighters* painted on the side.

She counted her team. "Where's Logan and Vince?"

"They went with that guy—what's his name, Crispin? Took off about a half hour ago." This from JoJo, who was pulling on her pack.

Wait. "They went…" Oh *no*. Of course he went after the nuke. And he'd needed guys to help carry it.

But the nuke was located…her breath caught, remembering the burn map.

"Jade, are you okay?" Finn came over.

She pressed her hands against her stomach, willing herself not to retch. Oh no, no…

No one died today. "See if you can get Logan on the radio." She took a breath. "Let's find a vehicle and get on the line. We have work to do." Lots of work. Focused, desperate work.

Finn had grabbed a radio, was reaching out to Logan.

She picked up a couple of saws, walked over to a nearby truck—Conner's. She recognized it from that day he'd rescued her from Crispin's place.

Oh, Crispin. She closed her eyes. *Please be alive.*

Because shoot, oh shoot—

"Chief. You don't look so hot." Finn had loaded in a couple shovels.

"Did you get ahold of Logan?"

"No dice. But I'll keep trying."

She nodded. "Do that."

Conner came out of the headquarters, kitted up in a pair of pants, boots, a jacket, helmet. "Where's the rest of your team?"

She stared at him. "I don't know. I...they might be in the fire."

He just blinked at her. "What?"

"Long story—"

"Okay, c'mon. I'll drop you on the line. We need to get the backfire started."

Yes. She'd start the fire, get it moving, then hand it over to her team.

Then she'd pray they were back, and if they weren't, she'd find them.

No one died today.

Please God.

Conner climbed into the cab.

She jumped into the back with JoJo, Finn, and Rico. Banged the back of the cab.

Conner took off, kicking up dirt out of the lot, down the street and over the bridge. She passed the parking lot of the doomed church and saw a number of people digging a line around the building.

That was hope, right there.

A flatbed sat on the side of the road, offloading another dozer. Conner pulled up to it, stuck his head out the window, gesturing. "Give me a thick link of dirt—all the way to the soil. No grass!"

Then he drove down the line and dropped off JoJo, and farther down, Rico, and finally Finn.

He stopped maybe fifty feet from the end. "I'll keep you posted. But you start that fire as soon as the dozer cuts the line."

"Yes, sir."

She hopped out, grabbed her Pulaski and drip torch. Here, the road veered away from the river, and a community park lay between the river and the highway. From the highway arched grassland until it hit the tree line, some fifty feet from the road.

She spotted a truck in the community parking lot and, while she waited for the dozer, ran across the road and into the lot. A rest area with bathrooms, swing sets, a play yard, a covered area with grills— she hoped the fire stopped before it took out this place.

Jogging up to the truck, something about it felt... wait.

Red dye splashed it, the cab, the bed, and...

She stopped. This truck belonged to The Brothers.

"Well, look who's here. If it isn't the trespasser."

She whirled around, her eyes wide.

Long hair, a beard, and he'd wiped his face free of the slurry but still wore it on his body, turning his skin blood red. Floyd, the man who'd been holding a gun on Crispin.

She got her Pulaski up, but not before he advanced on her and slapped her. Pain exploded through her face, her entire body, and she staggered. Her helmet fell off, and she hit a knee. He grabbed the axe and ripped it out of her hand. Threw it away.

"This is going to be fun."

Then he slammed his grip around her neck and backpedaled her to the truck.

She fought him, kicking, writhing, screaming, but Finn was working too far away to hear her.

Floyd opened up his back door and punched her again, and she whirled, her nose feeling lifted from her face, her jaw nearly dislocating. Blood spurted into the back area, and he shoved her in. Closed the door.

Then he rounded and got into the front.

Wait—*what?*

But as he roared away, as she curled into a ball, all she heard was her mother. *Survive today.*

He'd beaten the fire back to Snowhaven, but just barely. As they'd turned onto the road along the river, the black tumult of smoke billowed out of the forest to the north, the flames leaping from the haze of trees. A distant roar suggested it moved toward the town with ferocity.

"Bring us to the firehouse," Booth shouted from the back, where he sat with Vince and Logan, still securing Fanny. "We'll connect with our team from there."

Crispin couldn't help but search for Jade along the line of firefighters. They stood up to the fire, walking the edge with drip torches, lighting fires against a line of dirt plowed up by dozers peeling back the earth. The firefighters kept the fire away from the edge of the earth with shovelfuls of dirt, sometimes their own boots.

Above the chaos, planes offloaded water and the red stuff onto the blaze, but the aerial attack seemed fruitless.

Unless it was part of a master plan. Meanwhile, they fought the good fight with all they had, with the terrible hope that it would work.

He headed for the firehouse and found it nearly empty, all the firefighters deployed.

Booth and the guys jumped out of the back. He followed them inside the office.

163

Miles glanced up at them, on the phone. He hung up. "What are you guys doing here? You should be out on the line with your team."

He glanced at Crispin, then back at the men. "What happened?"

Oh, clearly he referred to their soaking-wet status.

"The fire caught us," Logan said. "We had to shelter in the lake."

A moment. Then, "You good to go back out?"

"Point us in the right direction," Logan said.

"Your team deployed along the far end of the road. They're lighting a backfire. Connect with Jade —she'll give you instructions." He picked up his phone again and turned back to watch the drone screen.

Crispin headed outside. "Let's offload Fanny." Probably the fire station was the right place to store her, for now.

Booth and Logan jumped up on the bed, Vince and Crispin took the protruding end, and they maneuvered the missile off the back, then carried it by the straps into the garage. Put a tarp over it and shoved it against the wall. It seemed the height of irresponsibility to leave it here, in the garage, but it was better than the woods. Still, as soon as he tracked down Jade, he'd call Sheriff Hutchinson, get a deputy up here while he waited for Thorne's man.

The firefighters went into the locker room to grab their gear, and Crispin pulled out his burner phone.

Dead, of course. Shoot. He needed to get ahold of Thorne, update him.

What he really wanted, however, was another go-round with Jade, this time with him getting his words in before she walked away. Like, *I'm sorry I didn't trust you.*

And maybe...*I don't want to be alone. Not anymore.*

Booth came out carrying a drip torch and a shovel, followed by Logan and Vince. They threw the gear into the back of the truck. "Let's move."

Crispin got into the cab and pulled out, heading back up the line.

The backfires had scorched the grass, started to build into the forest, the surface fuel expended. The smoke on the horizon billowed steam, gray smoke, the evidence the drops might be working.

Still, the closer the fire got, the more the entire earth seemed ablaze.

Booth banged on the cab, and he slowed as they reached one of the firefighters. A female, one of Jade's team. Logan leaned out, shouting. "Where's Jade?"

The woman pointed east. "End of the line."

Crispin nodded and kept driving, past another firefighter, then another. He spotted the end of the dozed trail, where the road met up with the mountain road he'd turned off from only fifteen minutes ago.

No Jade. He pulled over and Booth jumped out of the back, along with Logan and Vince.

"Where's Jade?" Logan said, standing in the road.

Crispin put the truck into Park and got out.

Vince and Booth ran across the road, holding drip torches. This area hadn't yet been burned, and they started it ablaze as Crispin searched for Jade.

Logan had crossed the road, had run up the small rise and now back, shaking his head.

Huh.

Crispin turned, looking at the parking lot, the river and—

There, in the lot, a yellow helmet. He sprinted over to it and picked it up. A fist hit his chest. *J. Ransom*, written in marker on the inside.

He turned, holding it, and another punch hit him when he spotted her axe.

Then, red slurry, dropped onto the pavement, a bloody stain.

No, oh *no*…

Maybe he was simply panicking. He ran out to the line, caught up with Booth. "I think Floyd has her."

Booth rounded. "What?"

"Yeah. This was in the lot." He held up her helmet. "And there's slurry on the pavement. His truck got doused."

Crispin's F-150 still dripped red.

Booth's look of horror probably mirrored his own. A beat, then, "Where would he take her?"

"I don't know."

"The 518 is blocked off—he couldn't get there. And all the back roads are burnt."

"The drone. Maybe we can find her with that."

Logan had come up, heard the conversation. Turned to Booth. "Go with him."

Oh. Crispin looked at Logan, the fire, back to Booth. Opened his mouth to protest, but…

But Booth was his partner. Perhaps it was time to remember that. "C'mon."

He headed to the truck, Booth on his tail.

Miles looked up at them as they barreled into his office. "What's going on?"

Okay, so maybe he looked like a man on fire. "Have you heard from Jade?"

Miles frowned. "No. I tried to raise her on the radio but got no answer. I figured she was working—why?"

"She's missing," Booth said.

"What?"

"I need the drone," Crispin said, walking over to the driver. "I need you to search the area for a white Silverado covered in red slurry."

"No," Miles said. "I need the drone coverage for the fire—"

"She's missing!" Crispin snapped. "She might even have been kidnapped by a terrorist!"

Miles eyes widened. "What—"

"Yes," Booth said, a lot more calmly. "Crispin—and I—have been hunting down a rogue terrorist group for the past couple months."

"What—"

"It's too long to explain," Crispin said. "But I need to find her." He turned back to the drone operator.

"What about her phone? Does she have it with her?" This from Miles.

"I don't know—maybe. Why?"

"You could track her GPS. I have her number." He thumbed open his contact list and then dialed. Listened, then put it on speakerphone.

"Hey. This is Jade. You know what to do—"

Miles hung up, his expression stark.

Nova came out of the locker room, into the office. "Hey, I found this in Jade's jumpsuit. I think she forgot it. It was ringing."

She held Jade's phone.

Crispin reached out for it, and she gave it to him.

He stared at the wallpaper on her phone. A poster of *Avengers: Infinity War*, of course, all the faces around a center A, ringed with light. She was such a pop-culture girl. X-Men. Avengers. *We match. Batman and Robin.*

He closed his eyes. *Where are you, Jade?*

No, better, *Lord, please, please help me find her.*

He listened, as if God might show up with an audible voice. Instead, there she was, Jade in his head, saying, *There's no fire that is worth the life of a teammate.*

And right behind that, a visual of her playing with that little black ring on her finger—oh my—

"What about her tracking system?"

"What tracking system?" Miles asked.

"She has a prototype of a system she's trying to develop to track lost firefighters. It connects to an app on her phone." He tried to open the phone, but a lock grid came up.

"Anyone know her code?"

Grimaces all around.

It was okay, he had a hack. He opened the emergency call feature and typed in random letters and numbers, then copy and pasted the text, over and over and over—

"What are you doing?" Booth said.

"That trick they taught us—"

"The crazy password trick?"

"What trick?" Nova asked.

"You get a ridiculously long password, like a hundred thousand characters, then paste it into the phone's password request. It crashes it." Booth said. "After a couple minutes, the phone reboots and opens an unlocked home screen."

"And we're in," Crispin said. He navigated to her app and opened it.

Wanted to weep. "It's working. The GPS has her —there's a big red dot." Widening the screen, he tried to place it—

Froze. "He's taken her back to my place," he said quietly.

"Why?"

He looked at Booth. "Because it's designed for a standoff. Provisions and weapons, cameras, and the outbuilding is a fortress. Maybe the people who sieged my place got a good look at it and reported in."

"Wow."

"Had to do something in my free time. But what he doesn't know is that I also know the vulnerabilities." He headed for the door. "After all, it is *my* bunker."

"I'm coming with you," Booth said, following him outside.

He turned, opened his mouth to argue, and then closed it. His throat thickened. After everything... "Thanks, Booth."

His old partner probably saw the emotion in his eyes. "We'll get her back, bro."

He hung on to Booth's words.

Because all he had was hope.

TWELVE

"It's not going to work. Crispin doesn't care about me. He's not coming for me."

She sat, her wrists secured by duct tape to the arms of a chair that Floyd had dragged from the house to the garage.

Or should she say *Batcave*, because while the rusted facade of corrugated metal siding gave the impression of neglect and disuse, behind the thin veneer of rust and flaking paint was a solid slab of ballistic steel, a thick concrete floor, a safe full of weapons, and a console of tech gear and screens.

To one side, a compact living quarters provided the bare necessities for a prolonged campout—a bunk with storage underneath, a fold-down table, and a small but efficient kitchenette. Tactical maps and blueprints plastered the walls, illuminated by focused task lighting. Crispin could start his own small war, or maybe stand off an army for a month, given the ammunition and MREs along with a propane-run stove. The place even contained a water supply in a massive hundred-gallon tank attached to the wall.

Hello, Crispin the super prepper. A few days ago

she might have accused him of believing too many conspiracy theories, but, well, they *had* found a nuke in the woods, stolen by terrorists who were working with Russians who'd wanted to blow it up in America, so...

Maybe not so much.

Floyd had gotten into the weapons cache and lined up a terrifying array of armament along the front of the garage, on either side of the door, where small windows acted as medieval arrow slits. He could shoot out but not be hit.

So, yeah, apparently they were sitting tight. Except, "He doesn't even know I'm gone."

Flatscreens on the wall showed the driveway in from the road as well as a thorough view of the yard.

Floyd set down his half-eaten MRE of corned beef hash, his spoon still in the bag, and rolled the office chair back from where he sat, watching said monitors.

He smelled of the woods, feral and rank, wore a pair of grimy fatigues, a sweat-sodden T-shirt under a vest, the arms shorn off. His long black hair and beard were still stained a little red, and his cold eyes bored a hole clear through her.

He emitted a laugh that sounded more like disgust than humor. "Sweetheart. Have you not been paying attention? Crispin is a hound dog with a bone. And you, darling, are the bone."

"Aside from that being a little gross, *you're* the one not paying attention. We barely know each other."

"I saw you at the compound. With him. And I know you were here before. My guys sent me photos. I know him. Guys like him work alone. Unless—"

SUSAN MAY WARREN

"We're just friends." She cut him off before he could be rude. "Barely friends, really. More like…"

Pardners. She looked away, hating the word suddenly in her heart, her throat. Aw, now her eyes burned.

C'mon, she was tougher than this.

"We are nothing to each other," she said tightly, her gaze on him.

A tear escaped, but she didn't break her glare.

"We'll see." He turned back to the MRE. "My money is on Crispin being the hero again." He winked, and she felt dirty to her soul.

She closed her eyes. *Please, God…*

She didn't know what to pray for. Because, in her wildest, deepest places, yes, she wanted Crispin to burst through the door, take out Floyd, sweep her up and…

Shoot. Rescue her.

She let out a breath. Stared at the corrugated ceiling. She was tired of being tough. Her brother was right. Maybe she did have something to prove.

That her scars didn't matter to her. That she didn't need to be seen as a victim. That she didn't need to be protected.

But Crispin—he'd taken all that apart, hadn't he? He'd called her capable and smart. The toughest woman he knew. *Has it occurred to you that maybe your wounds are only proof of that?*

And sure, she'd told herself that for years…but maybe it hadn't reached her heart. Because if it had, she wouldn't so easily walk away from a man who saw her as beautiful.

Breathtakingly beautiful.

So maybe being protected didn't mean weak. Or

incapable. And maybe trusting God meant not running away from love but trusting God to also protect her heart as well as her body and soul.

She closed her eyes. *I know, God, You can deliver me from this, if it's Your will. And if You want to use Crispin, I...I'll trust You.*

Survive today. She opened her eyes.

Floyd watched the monitors, his attention focused.

Which meant she could probably get her arms free. Except, what then?

The lights went out. Just like that, darkness flooded the room, save for the pinpricks of light through the slotted windows.

Floyd roared, the metal rolling chair sounding as he got up.

She ripped one arm up toward her chest, breaking the tape. Then the other.

Smoke filled the room, maybe deployed through one of the arrow slits, but she rolled out of the chair and onto the floor to get away from it.

Shots fired, Floyd manning one of the weapons at the window.

She scampered away from the propane tank, toward the bunk.

Scrabbling sounded on the roof even as shots fired into the slotted window. Floyd swore. She rolled into a ball, protecting herself just as a door in the roof opened.

As if he might be Batman himself, Crispin dropped into the smoky room. He wore body armor, goggles, and dropped Floyd with one shot.

She didn't even have time to scream.

Just like that—*what?*—it was over. She still had

her hands pressed to her ears when Crispin crouched in front of her.

Another man dropped behind him, but her eyes stayed on her superhero.

He crouched in front of her, and for a second, his gaze roamed her face, wincing, maybe at her injuries. Then he smiled tightly. "Hey there, Tough Girl."

She launched into his arms, hard, knocking him back, but he caught her in his embrace, holding her so tight her breath left her.

"I didn't think you even knew I was gone—" she said, and now her voice broke. "How did you find me?"

"Your ring." His voice emerged a little hitched. "I found your phone in your pants. Apparently, it's a habit."

She laughed and leaned back, stared at his solemn expression. "I'm sorry I didn't listen to you. I was scared that—"

"That you were going to get burned by a guy who didn't realize how much he needed you."

Oh. That. "I know I can be bossy, and maybe I do have to prove myself sometimes, but I hate being the weak link, and—"

"Just shut up and let me rescue you."

Then he kissed her. A solid rescuer's kiss that did very much shut her up.

He tasted of smoke and fire, of passion and desire, and most of all…hope.

No. *More* than hope. Tomorrow, and three days after that. And three more after that…

She grabbed his body armor and held him there, kissing him back, until behind them, someone cleared his throat.

She looked up over at the man. Booth.

"So, we do have a fire to fight."

Oh, that.

"Sheesh, Booth. Give a guy a moment to just breathe."

"Save it, Crispin. I know you don't breathe." Then Booth walked over to the door and hit the opener.

The door rose, and sweet air rushed into the darkness, light illuminating Floyd's body in the corner.

All his menace, gone just like that.

Crispin helped her up, then keyed in the garage code to close the door, Floyd left in the darkness. "We'll deal with him later. We need to get you back to the fire. They need you."

Except, did they? She stopped him, right there in the driveway. "No. They don't. Jed is there, and so are Conner and Miles and a host of other firefighters, and yes, let's go help, but...they don't need *me*. They need all of us. That's the only way we put out the fires in our lives. With our team. Our partners."

He met her gaze, then glanced at Booth, back to her. "Yes."

She rose up to kiss him again —

"Nope, nope, we need to keep moving, Chief," Booth said.

She laughed. "Fine." But the expression Crispin wore definitely said...*later*.

Crispin peeled off his body armor and tossed it in the back of his truck, next to Booth's. Then he got in the driver's seat. She scooted into the middle, Booth next to the passenger door.

Crispin put the truck into Drive, pulled out. And

that's when she noticed he still wore the T-shirt from the hospital.

"We're definitely going to have to get you a new shirt," she said. "One that says Jude County firefighter."

"I'm not a firefighter," he said, pulling out into the road.

"That's what you think." Then she wrapped her hand around his arm — nice biceps — and smiled.

And he thought chasing down terrorists was hard.

Crispin climbed out of the back of the fire truck, driven by Logan, and fell into the grimy ranks of too many hotshots and smokejumpers to count. And really, they all simply looked like a sooty blur against the clutter of smoke and ash and...victory.

Twenty-four hours of fighting the fire as it crested down the mountain, water hoses streaming from the river, dirt thrown on spot fires, and so very much digging as fire tried to escape over the line.

His bones wanted to crumble. Instead, he spotted Jade, equally as blackened, talking with a taller man. Frankly, everyone looked alike here, all in yellow jackets, names blurred by soot, their faces plastered in sweat and dirt.

But he could make out Jade anywhere, like a homing beacon.

Yes, that was right. A homing beacon, because around her the world stopped being a foreign, angry, dangerous place.

He wanted more than three days. He'd take forever, please.

But for now, "Hey."

She smiled at him. "You look terrible."

"What?" He pushed his helmet up. Miles had issued him pants, boots, a jacket, a hat. "That's the pot. Besides, I've had worse."

She laughed. "Yeah. The soot covers up all the bruises."

"Bruises?" This from the tall man beside her.

"Crispin, this is my brother, Jed."

"Oh, the famous hotshot brother."

The man gave him a raised-eyebrow look.

"Please," Crispin said. "Apparently you're the town hero."

"Word on the street is I've been dethroned by a guy who hunts down terrorists and rogue nukes."

"Really. Sounds like trouble. Zero stars, would not recommend." But Crispin smiled.

"By the way, where is Fanny?" Jade asked.

"I got ahold of Thorne when we got back, while you headed back out to the line. Waited around and eventually his men came to get it. A guy named York and another guy, Pete. Don't worry—they showed me creds. And they arrived with Sheriff Hutchinson, so I let them take Fanny."

"I'm not worried."

"You're a little worried."

She shrugged. "Fanny and I had a bond. Didn't want her hooking up with just anyone." She winked. "We should check on Henry."

He liked the *we* in that sentence. He glanced at Jed. "By the way, the real hero is Brains McChurchill here, with her Normandy-style attack on the fire." He held out his fist.

Jade bumped it. Beamed at him.

"I agree," Jed said, then put a hand on her helmet. "There's a new Ransom in town."

"Not for long," she said.

The words punched him. Just a full-out, full-body blow, center mass.

Wait—*what?*

He'd thought—except, she hadn't said she was sticking around. Ever.

"Oh, are you leaving?" He was trying, very hard, to keep his voice light. No problem, no knife to the heart here.

She looked at him, her eyes widening. "Um. I mean…now that the fire's out…"

"Oh. I thought…" And he didn't know why the words felt like they'd been raked out of his soul. Shoot. He looked away.

"Was that my motorcycle I saw at the Ember station?" Jed said.

Jade made a face.

And then he got it. *Jed.*

Maybe there was only room for one Ransom in town.

So he took a breath and went for broke. "I've never been to Alaska…"

She studied his face, so much emotion in her eyes. "It's dangerous," she said quietly, "and wild. And a person can pretty much get lost and start over there."

"I could like that."

She smiled.

And oh, he really wanted to get her alone.

"I need to get going," Jed said.

She turned to him. "You should stick around Ember. There's chatter about a blowout barbecue tomorrow night."

"I think we just had that," Crispin said, breathing again.

"Right," she laughed. "No. With food from the Hotline, and maybe cupcakes, and even talk about getting Oaken Fox to show back up and play some music."

Not exactly the night he'd planned, but in his mind, he was already building them a cabin under the northern lights. So, "I could probably stay awake for that."

"I'll see you back at the house, sis," Jed said and gave Crispin a side-eye.

He wasn't that guy. Ever, but especially now. So he held out his hand. "Good to meet you, Jed. I'll make sure she gets home safely."

Jed eyed her, then smiled and shook his head as he walked away.

"What was that about?" she said.

"Just a short conversation about how you're amazing and pretty much blew him away, but also how I shouldn't get any big ideas because he's watching and is pretty sure he can read my mind. And he's right."

Her eyes widened. Her back was to the wall, and he braced a hand over her shoulder and bent down. "But you're safe with me."

"Please. I know better." But she wore laughter in her eyes. "And I like it."

A deep rumble came from inside him. His gaze went to her mouth. "'Spose we can get him to loan you his bike?"

"We'll probably have to steal it."

"I'm okay with that."

She laughed. "Oh, you *are* trouble."

"What happened to Tough Guy?"

"Oh, him. I'm onto him. He's actually just a big softie." Then she rose on her toes and kissed him. Quickly. Sweetly.

He barely stopped himself from sweeping her up, but not here, not in front of her team. He let her keep it chaste.

"Don't let it get around," he said as she lowered herself back down.

"It might be too late." She pointed at her team, clustered around a grimy truck. Booth gave him a thumbs-up.

"Listen." She patted his chest. "We can stop in and see Henry on the way back to Ember. But I need to wrap up things with Miles first. And oh boy, you need a shower." She lifted her hand and touched his forehead. "You're bleeding. Are you wounded?"

"Absolutely. Could be life-threatening. I think maybe I need a doctor. Or a smokejumper."

"Oh brother. A guy will say anything to get me to rescue him."

"Anything."

She laughed. "Crispin."

"That's Crispy to you there, Chief. Now kiss me and make it all better."

"Bossy."

"Right."

So she did.

EPILOGUE

The Hotline was already rockin' when Jade showed up on Jed's bike. Cars jammed the dirt lot, the enticing lure of smoked ribs tugging her inside, along with a cover from one of Ben King's country hits.

The twangy sounds, the deep vocals filled the air as she walked inside, the cadre of smokejumpers, hotshots, and locals loud, some singing along, a few on the dance floor, booths crowded, chairs scattered at random tables, and a few familiar faces shooting pool.

The Ember vibe she remembered. Jade slid into a booth beside Nova and stole a French fry from her basket.

Nova glanced over her shoulder and grinned. "Hey, you."

"How's the ankle?"

"Good enough to dance, if Booth decides to show up." She turned on the stool. "He's with Crispin, talking with Henry."

"I don't know how to get ahold of Crispin. His phone took a dip in the river."

"I heard about that." Nova reached for her glass of soda. "Still can't believe we stopped it."

"The fire?"

Nova raised an eyebrow.

"Oh, the other thing."

"Booth filled me in. Hard to believe that Floyd was an international terrorist connected with Russians." Nova took a sip of soda, put it on the counter. "But it's Montana. Anything happens here."

"Oh, it's the little brother to Alaska. You want crazy terrorists hiding in the woods, you try jumping with the Midnight Sun smokejumpers. We've walked into fields of marijuana, nests of rogue militia, and even spooked a couple runaway prisoners out of hiding." She motioned to the barkeep and pointed at the basket of fries for herself.

"Does that mean you're staying?" Nova ran a fry around ketchup.

She cast a look past her to the dance floor. "Hey, is that…" No, it couldn't be— "That looks like the actor Spenser Storm." He was dancing with a pretty blonde. She looked familiar.

Nova followed her gesture. "Oh, yeah. He was here filming a movie earlier this summer. He met Emily on set. Actually, he reported the ignition of the original blaze. A cabin that blew up."

"Really? I remember watching him as a kid in *Trek of the Osprey*."

"Me too. And the guy on the stage—Oaken Fox. He did music for the movie."

She spotted the man, dark-blond hair, wearing a pair of jeans and a flannel shirt, his low voice leaning into the mic. "Right. He did a reality show recently—something about joining a rescue team in Alaska."

"Well, once upon a time, I might have let him rescue me, but…"

"But you have Booth," Jade said. The barkeep handed her a water, a straw. "Thanks." She unsheathed the straw and put it in the water, took a drink. Her throat still burned a little from yesterday's fight with the flames. They'd gotten back to Ember last night, and she'd taken a shower and then fallen into a dead sleep for twelve full hours. When she rose, she discovered a note in the kitchen from Jed, inviting her to stay.

Sweet, but…no.

Probably not.

Except…well, maybe after twenty-four hours, the drama of the fire and the intensity of what had gone down between her and Crispin might have worn off. She didn't want to lean too hard into his suggestion about Alaska.

"I'm a little afraid that maybe Henry is talking Booth and Crispin into something…more…" Nova said, staring at her fries. "Although, Booth did say he wanted to stick around, so…"

"I get it," Jade said. "Crispin said he might want to follow me to Alaska, but…that's crazy, right? I mean, we barely know each other. At least you've known Booth for years."

"He drove me crazy for years, really."

"Crazy good?" Jade said.

Nova smiled. "Maybe. But I know all this hero stuff speaks to him, so…"

Jade lifted her glass. "We wouldn't want them any other way."

Nova tapped hers against Jade's. "You said it."

She took a sip, then set her glass down. "So, will you still go to Alaska if Crispin doesn't?"

Her foxhole prayer rose inside her, about God delivering her and using Crispin to do it.

Three days, and three days more. And Jed had invited her to stay.

"I love Alaska, but…"

Nova slid off the stool, lifting her hand, and Jade turned to see Booth coming into the Hotline. Nova grabbed his hand, then put her arms around his neck.

So, the former team lead was clearly off duty.

And then Crispin came in behind him.

Oh, the man could eclipse a room with his dark, heady good looks. And when his gaze roamed the room and landed on her, her heart nearly stood still.

Yep, three days and she was a goner. Oh boy.

He walked past Nova and Booth and over to her. Slid onto Nova's empty stool. "Hey there, Sparky."

She raised an eyebrow. He laughed. And oh, it washed over her, warm, deep, and found root inside. Something had changed over the last twenty-four hours. He'd shucked away the desperation, the earnestness, the laser focus on his mission, maybe. And when he smiled, it touched his beautiful eyes, sparked something in them.

Or…oh no. Wait. "What happened with Henry?"

He motioned to the bartender and ordered a root beer. Turned back to her. "Henry is going to be fine. But…I have bad news."

She knew it. Her throat tightened, her chest suddenly hot. "He gave you another assignment, didn't he?"

He stared at her a moment, then…laughed?

What? "Sort of. But I'm dead, remember? And the bad news is that I probably have to stay dead."

"Are you in danger?"

"Maybe. The Petrov Bratva has long arms. But…I have a plan."

The bartender slid his drink over. He took it. Took a sip. "Oh, I love old-fashioned root beer."

"Crispin!"

The voice came from over his shoulder, and he turned as a woman came running up to him. Pretty, with her hair pulled back, wearing a white shirt and jeans, cowboy boots, she threw her arms around Crispin.

He'd gotten up, set his drink down, and now pulled her up against himself.

Behind her stood Houston James, one of the hotshots. She'd met him briefly during mop-up. Nice guy, he wore scars from his own wrestle with fire, so she felt a sort of kinship with him. Now, he shoved his hands into his jeans, watching the two embrace. Wore a smile.

She did the quick math and came up with— Crispin's sister?

He set her down and put his arm over her shoulder, even as he reached out a hand to Houston. "Good to see you again."

Then he turned to Jade and confirmed. "This is Sophie Lamb, my sister."

Sophie held out her hand, her eyes warm. "Hey. I hear you're a smokejumper."

Jade nodded. "I'm from Alaska. Came down for the big fire. And the barbecue afterparty."

Sophie laughed, and it sounded like Crispin's, and Jade immediately liked her.

Jade's fries arrived and she reached for the ketchup.

"We'll catch up later, Soph," Crispin said as Houston took her hand. "Looks like your preacher wants to dance with you."

"Preacher?" Jade asked as Crispin sat back on the stool. She shoved the fries toward him.

"He was a youth pastor back in Last Chance County." He glanced again at his sister. "And they had a thing there, years ago. He's not the same guy she left behind." He turned to Jade. "But finding the right woman can do that."

Her eyes widened. "Do what?"

"Make a man look at his life. Ask what he wants."

Oh.

"And…" She swallowed. "And what do you want, Crispin?"

He smiled then and leaned close to her. "I want to get out of here."

Oh.

"Jed let you take out his bike?"

She nodded.

"Wanna let me drive?"

She smiled. "Yeah."

He motioned to the bartender, who came over. Crispin pulled a twenty out of his pocket, handed it over, and asked for a bag for the fries. He dumped them in, handed the bag to her, and took her hand.

Outside, the sun still hung against the northwest mountains, casting a fiery twilight across the town of Ember and into the parking lot.

He held out his hand and she gave him the key. He climbed on and she settled in behind him, her hand on his waist.

"C'mon, you can do better than that," he said, and she leaned in, put her arm around him.

"Hold on tighter." Then he peeled out of the lot.

She laughed. Clearly this was his MO, mission or not. Ernest, driven, high action. But his words returned to her.

Henry had sort of given him a mission?

Oh. She hung on tighter. Because if he was officially dead, the freedom it gave him to live life in the shadows, rooting out evil, saving the world…

The hero stuff speaks to him…

So she'd hang on while she could.

He drove them out of town and along the back roads that wound through the woods and up a mountain, and finally pulled up to a dirt lot with a trailhead sign.

"Where are we?"

He just held out his hand to help her off. Then laced his fingers through hers and headed for the trailhead. A thin path led through the forest, not far, and after a moment, they came out to a ranger fire tower.

"What's this?" she asked as she climbed up the stairs that led to a small platform. It wound around the building. Unmanned, although the inside held a small cot and communication equipment.

"I always wanted to come up here," he said. "You can see it from the highway, and I thought the view would be perfect."

She stood at the rail. Indeed. From here, the world stretched for hundreds of miles, mountain upon mountain, with the valley below still lush and green. The twilight had deepened, dark purple in the heavens, just a glow of orange light in the valley. And against the pane of sky, white droplets. "It's breathtaking."

"Yes," he said, and the husky tenor of his voice made her turn. He stood right behind her and now parked his hands on her hips, met her eyes, desire in them. "Breathtaking."

Oh. Her mouth dried. She put her hands on his chest. "You're destined to break my heart, aren't you, Crispy?"

One side of his mouth tweaked up. Then, "Why is that?"

"Because you have a new mission, don't you?" She couldn't look at him, so instead focused her gaze on his chest, that well in his neck where the smallest patch of hair peeked out from it. He hadn't shaved, so he wore a small layer of dark grizzle too. But he'd showered, because the delicious scent of soap lifted off him.

"I do," he said quietly. And her eyes closed. She knew it.

But his hand caught her chin, raised her head.

"Open your eyes, Jade. I want to see your eyes."

Oh, she refused to cry. She'd managed this long without him —

His hazel-green gaze searched hers. Then, "Jade, don't you already know?"

She frowned, shook her head.

"Sparky, my new mission is you."

Her mouth opened.

"I'm going to Alaska. Not to hide, and not to die, but to live." He smiled then. "Somebody has to keep you alive."

"So the Sparky thing is staying?"

"Probably. We'll see."

She laughed. "I think I'm the one keeping you alive."

He leaned in, his voice close to her ear. "Yes, Jade. Yes, you are."

Then he kissed her. Sweetly. Perfectly. Deeply. Taking his time, as if forever stretched out ahead of them.

And as the stars settled around her and the moon came out to light their path, she knew it did.

BONUS EPILOGUES

FLASHPOINT—FLASHOVER—FLASHBACK—FIRESTORM—FIRELINE

Want to know what your favorite Chasing Fire: Montana couples are up to? You can receive a special gift, available only to our newsletters subscribers. These **Bonus Epilogues** are not available on any retailer platform—they are only available to Sunrise newsletter subscribers.

BONUS EPILOGUES

Get your free gift, which includes bonus epilogues for Emily and Spenser, Sophie and Houston, Allie and Dakota, Jayne and Charlie, and Nova and Booth, by scanning the QR code below. Unsubscribe at any time.

Happy reading!

Have you read each Chasing Fire: Montana romantic adventure?

DON'T MISS ANY CHASING FIRE: MONTANA STORIES

With heart-pounding excitement, gripping suspense, and sizzling (but clean!) romance, the CHASING FIRE: MONTANA series, brought to you by the incredible authors of Sunrise Publishing, including the dynamic duo of bestselling authors Susan May Warren and Lisa Phillips, is your epic summer binge read.

Immerse yourself in a world of short, captivating novels that are designed to be devoured in one sitting. Each book is a standalone masterpiece, (no story cliffhangers!) although you'll be craving the next one in the series!

Follow the Montana Hotshots and Smokejumpers as they chase a wildfire through northwest Montana.

ELITE GUARDIANS: SAVANNAH

Safety. Secrets. Sacrifice. What will it cost these Elite Guardians to protect the innocent? Discover the answers in our Elite Guardians: Savannah series.

DISCOVER OUR LAST CHANCE FIRE AND RESCUE SERIES

FIRE. FAMILY. FAITH.
LAST CHANCE FIRE AND RESCUE

Dive into this thrilling first responder series now!

MORE ADVENTURE AWAITS...

SCAN OUR QR CODE FOR MORE ROMANTIC SUSPENSE!

ABOUT SUSAN MAY WARREN

With nearly 2 million books sold, critically acclaimed novelist Susan May Warren is the Christy, RITA, and Carol award-winning author of over ninety-five novels with Tyndale, Barbour, Steeple Hill, and Summerside Press. Known for her compelling plots and unforgettable characters, Susan has written contemporary and historical romances, romantic-suspense, thrillers, rom-com, and Christmas novellas.

With books translated into eight languages, many of her novels have been ECPA and CBA bestsellers, were chosen as Top Picks by *Romantic Times*, and have won the RWA's Inspirational Reader's Choice contest and the American Christian Fiction Writers Book of the Year award. She's a three-time RITA finalist and an eight-time Christy finalist.

Publishers Weekly has written of her books, "Warren lays bare her characters' human frailties, including fear, grief, and resentment, as openly as she details their virtues of love, devotion, and resiliency. She has crafted an engaging tale of romance, rivalry, and the power of forgiveness." *Library Journal* adds, "Warren's characters are well-developed and she knows how to create a first rate contemporary romance..."

Susan is also a nationally acclaimed writing coach, teaching at conferences around the nation, and winner of the 2009 American Christian Fiction Writers Mentor of the Year award. She loves to help people launch their writing careers. She is the founder of www.MyBookTherapy.com and www.learnhow-towriteanovel.com, a writing website that helps authors get published and stay published. She is also the author of the popular writing method *The Story Equation*.

Find excerpts, reviews, and a printable list of her novels at www.susanmaywarren.com and connect with her on social media.

facebook.com/susanmaywarrenfiction

instagram.com/susanmaywarren

x.com/susanmaywarren

bookbub.com/authors/susan-may-warren

goodreads.com/susanmaywarren

amazon.com/Susan-May-Warren

CONNECT WITH SUNRISE

Thank you again for reading *Fireproof*. We hope you enjoyed the story. If you did, would you be willing to do us a favor and leave a review? It doesn't have to be long—just a few words to help other readers know what they're getting. (But no spoilers! We don't want to wreck the fun!) Thank you again for reading!

We'd love to hear from you—not only about this story, but about any characters or stories you'd like to read in the future. Contact us at www.sunrisepublishing.com/contact.

We also have a monthly update that contains sneak peeks, reviews, upcoming releases, and fun stuff for our reader friends. Sign up at www.sunrisepublishing.com or scan our QR code.

MORE EPIC ROMANTIC ADVENTURE

CHASING FIRE: MONTANA

Flashpoint by Susan May Warren

Flashover by Megan Besing

Flashback by Michelle Sass Aleckson

Firestorm by Lisa Phillips

Fireline by Kate Angelo

Fireproof by Susan May Warren

MONTANA FIRE BY SUSAN MAY WARREN

Where There's Smoke (Summer of Fire)

Playing with Fire (Summer of Fire)

Burnin' For You (Summer of Fire)

Oh, The Weather Outside is Frightful (Christmas novella)

I'll be There (Montana Fire/Deep Haven crossover)

Light My Fire (Summer of the Burning Sky)

The Heat is On (Summer of the Burning Sky)

Some Like it Hot (Summer of the Burning Sky)

You Don't Have to Be a Star (spin-off)

LAST CHANCE FIRE AND RESCUE BY LISA PHILLIPS

Expired Return

Expired Hope (with Megan Besing)

Expired Promise (with Emilie Haney)

Expired Vows (with Laura Conaway)

LAST CHANCE COUNTY BY LISA PHILLIPS

Expired Refuge

Expired Secrets

Expired Cache

Expired Hero

Expired Game

Expired Plot

Expired Getaway

Expired Betrayal

Expired Flight

Expired End

Made in the USA
Columbia, SC
18 September 2024